WOLF
RIDER

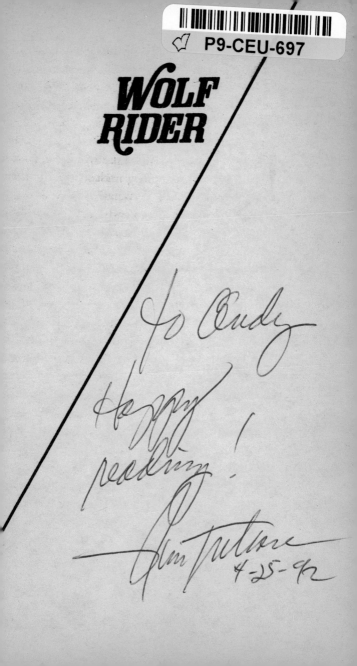

To Andy

Happy
reading!

Jim Tutcore
4-25-92

WOLF RIDER

A Tale of Terror

by AVI

Collier Books
Macmillan Publishing Company
New York

Collier Books
Macmillan Publishing Company
866 Third Avenue, New York, NY 10022
Collier Macmillan Canada, Inc.

First Collier Books edition 1988
Printed in the United States of America
A hardcover edition of Wolf Rider is available from
Bradbury Press, an affiliate of Macmillan, Inc.

10   9

Library of Congress Cataloging-in-Publication Data
Avi, 1937- Wolf rider.
Summary: After receiving an apparent crank call from a
man claiming to have committed murder, fifteen-year-old
Andy finds his close relationship with his father
crumbling as he struggles to make everyone believe him.
[1. Fathers and sons—Fiction.   2. Mystery and
detective stories]   1. Title.
PZ7.A953Wo   1988   [Fic]   87-23905
ISBN 0-02-041511-7

For David Hipschman

**WOLF
RIDER**

Part One

The kitchen phone rang three times before Andy picked it up. "Hello?" he said.

A voice replied, "I just killed someone."

"What?"

"I just killed someone."

"I don't understand," said Andy.

"I have to tell . . ."

"Who is this?" Andy demanded.

"I killed Nina."

"You killed . . . Nina," Andy echoed. From across the kitchen his friend Paul—who had just arrived—was staring at him. They were on their way to a party.

The voice said, "What should I do?" It was a male voice, low, flat.

Andy pulled a chair over to the table and sat down. He said into the phone, "I don't get it."

"I killed her," the voice continued. "Now I don't know what to do." Andy could recognize no accent.

Again he said, "Who is this?"

"Zeke."

"Zeke *who*?"

"Zeke."

Andy sat up very straight. "Is this some joke?" he demanded. "It's not very funny. Who *is* this?"

"I don't know what to do," said the voice. "I loved her."

From across the room Paul whispered, "What's going on?"

Andy pointed to the paper and pencil that lay on the kitchen counter. When Paul didn't seem to understand, Andy snapped his fingers as well as pointed. Nodding, Paul slid paper and pencil to him. Into the phone, Andy said, "But you did it."

"Yeah," the voice returned. "I stabbed her."

"Stabbed her . . . ," Andy said. It made him queasy to say the words. "When?"

"Just now."

"Why?" asked Andy. On the paper he wrote:

Guy killed someone
Go outside phone
Call cops. Trace call to 771-1416
I'll try to keep him on

He shoved the message at Paul.

"I got angry at her," said Zeke.

"Angry," Andy repeated, watching Paul read the note and wishing he would act.

"I wanted to go out with her," Zeke continued, "but she didn't want to. So I killed her. What should I do?"

Paul, finally grasping what Andy was telling him, mouthed the word "okay" and bolted out the front door. Andy sat back, determined to hang on until help came.

/ The man who said he was Zeke could see the body in front of him. She was lying on the floor as though asleep. She no longer moved. She no longer made sounds. The bright yellow sweater she wore was blotched with blood, and there was blood on the floor. But her eyes remained open. To Zeke's eyes there was something peaceful about what he saw. Nina was no longer mocking him, no longer indifferent.

Just the thought of that made him angry again. He was glad he had punished her, made her feel the way he felt when she ignored him. Numb. Cold.

But he felt puzzled, as if he were seeing himself from a distance. It was important for him to explain to someone why he felt such anger when he punished Nina. . . .

/ "I'm not sure what I should do," Zeke said into the phone, his voice soft, persistent.

Andy said, "Maybe if you talk to me I'll get an idea."

"Yes," Zeke agreed. "That would be good."

Andy picked up his pencil. "Where are you now?" he asked.

"Her house."

Andy got ready to write it down. "Where's that?"

There was a slight hesitation. "In town."

"Anyone else there?"

"Just her. And she's not really here, is she?"

"How come you called me?" said Andy.

"Needed to talk to someone. I just dialed her phone. You mind I called you?"

Andy worked spit into his dry mouth. "No, sure. It's okay. Go ahead."

"I was feeling lonely," said Zeke. "You ever get that way? Restless. Jumpy. Can't sit still. So I came to her house. It's a long walk. Too far. I kept thinking about her and what we were going to do."

"She expecting you?" asked Andy.

"No. I just came here."

"What's her name?"

"I told you. Nina."

Andy wrote it down. "Nina . . . what?"

"Nina . . . Klemmer."

"She a friend?"

"Sort of."

"What happened when you got there?"

"She has a car. A red Ford. An Escort. I don't have a car. Wish I did. Maybe it wouldn't have happened. A car does good things for me. Lets me get away. It's so flat around here. Where I come from, you have hills. Mountains. But here!

You walk and you walk and you still don't get anywhere. *Ever.* I said to her, 'Let's go dancing.' But she said, 'No, I don't want to.' Said she was going out with someone else. Didn't want anything to do with me. That made me mad. I'm a great dancer. I went into her kitchen and got a knife. And I killed her. Stabbed her."

"You killed her . . . ," Andy echoed, feeling sick again. When he swallowed it hurt.

"Should I bury her in the backyard?" Zeke asked. "Or should I go away and leave her? I don't know what to do. I'm mixed up. She's just lying here bleeding. No, not anymore. Just a pool of blood."

"Do you want to call the police?" asked Andy.

"No."

"Why?"

"I'm scared. Wouldn't you be scared if you'd killed someone? Wouldn't you?"

"I guess . . ."

"They'd put me in jail. Mess me up. Do all sorts of things to me. Know what I mean?"

"Tell me about . . . Nina."

"She's very pretty. I mean . . . she *was* very pretty. She dressed fantastic. Perfect. Beautiful. She isn't pretty now. She was always pale. Now she's more pale. I'm sort of sorry. She has . . . had . . . black hair. Dyed, I think. Dark eyes. Red, red lipstick. Bright fingernails. About five feet six. And thin. I can see her now. Really, if you had seen her, you'd agree. Beautiful."

"But you killed her . . ."

"She used to make fun of me. Ignore me. But when she saw me with the knife, she got frightened. Said she'd go out with me then. Begged me not to kill her. Started to cry. I mean, sobbing, coughing. Her face got ugly. But it was too late. I was angry. I had to punish her."

On the phone line Andy heard a series of clicks.

"What's that?" Zeke asked.

"What?" said Andy.

"Those clicks?"

Andy was certain the clicks meant the police were tracing the call. "Tell me more," he said.

After a moment Zeke said: "Think I should leave her?"

"No."

"How come?"

"I think . . . you better talk to me."

"You glad I called?" Zeke asked.

"It's okay."

"You're good to talk to. What's your name?"

"Pete," said Andy.

"Pete what?"

"Pete Smith. Where does Nina live?"

"I'm not sure."

"How come?"

"Sometimes I don't remember things. Sometimes I even forget who I am. Think I'm someone else . . ."

"Do you remember where you met her?"

"She's a student."

"Where?"

"At . . . the college."

"The one in town?"

"I guess."

"You a student?"

"No way."

"And you're sorry you killed her."

"I never said that. I'm just mixed up about what to do. And besides . . ."

There was another series of clicks on the line, then the phone went dead.

"Hello!" Andy cried. "Zeke? Hello!"

Andy slowly hung up the phone and leaned forward to rest his head on the cool white surface of the kitchen table. "Jesus," he whispered, feeling nauseous. "Oh, Jesus . . ."

/ The man who called himself Zeke looked at the phone for a long time. Then with a sigh he got up, walked from the room and out of the house.

/ Though his hands shook, Andy made himself start writing down everything Zeke had told him, concentrating so hard that when the doorbell chimes rang he jumped. It was Paul. Andy let him in.

"What's happening?" Paul demanded.

"Wait a minute," Andy said and hurried back to the table. Only when he was done did he fling the pencil down, exhausted.

Paul watched him. Finally he said, "That for real?"

Andy shut his eyes. "It sounded real. You get to a phone?"

"Went to the main road," Paul began. "You know, where the fire station is. Guys sitting around. When I told them it was an emergency, they said I could use their phone. Called the operator. Told *her* it was an emergency. But when I reached the cops and told them what you said, guess what?"

"Paul . . ."

"The cop laughed."

"*Laughed?*"

"Said it was a gag."

"What about tracing the call?"

"Said it was hard to do that. Only easy on TV."

Frustrated, Andy looked away.

"Hey, listen," Paul continued. "Then the cop said, 'Don't worry, son. It's a full moon, Friday night, and welfare checks just out. Forget it.' "

"Paul, the call . . ."

"Know what I'm saying? Sucker didn't think he could. But, you know, he'd try. Good thing you gave me your new number."

"Maybe they did trace it," said Andy. "I heard some odd clicks." He went into the living room, which was crowded with still-packed boxes. Pushing a lamp to one side, he sat heavily on the couch.

"You all right?" Paul asked.

"Yes," Andy said, but he felt cold.

"Andy . . ."

"What?"

"What did the guy say?"

Andy told him.

$/$ "Hey," Paul said at last. "No way. Can't be serious."

Andy went to the phone and pushed the operator button. "Police, please," he said. To Paul he said, "I better talk to them."

"Madison Police. Officer Seneto speaking. May I be of some assistance?"

"My name is Andy . . . Andrew Zadinski. We just moved from across town. I live with my father, Dr. Robert Zadinski. He teaches at the college. Look, this guy just called me. Said he killed someone. I had my friend call so you could trace him."

"Oh, right. Sure. I took it."

"Did you trace him?"

"Afraid not, son. It's not so easy to do. He hung up much too fast."

Andy said, "I wrote down everything he told me. I've got it here. Want to hear?"

"Okay. If it's not too much, go ahead."

After Andy repeated it all, the policeman said, "That it?"

"Yes, sir."

"Okay, son," he said. "Don't worry. We'll take care of it."

"Sir," said Andy, "when you learn for sure,

would you let me know what happened? I'd like to know. My number's 771-1416. It's a new listing."

"No problem. Thanks for calling. Have a good night."

Andy held on to the receiver. "They'll call when they learn something," he said, as much to himself as to Paul.

"Hey, remember when we were kids?" said Paul. "We'd call and ask stupid questions. A joke. That's all it was."

"Sounded real."

Paul shrugged. "We going to the party?"

Andy hung up the phone. "Let me put my head back on," he said.

/ In the small bathroom next to his room Andy ran cold water over his head and neck. As he dried his hair he looked at himself in the mirror, staring into his own eyes for a long time.

He was tall, a still-growing fifteen. His face was long, his nose slightly bent from wrestling roughhouse when he was eight. His eyes were dark and he had reddish brown hair, which he kept neat. "They'll take care of it," he said to himself.

Paul called from the front room.

"Be right there!" Andy returned. But first he stepped into his father's room, which was as cluttered with cartons as the rest of the apartment. The phone answering machine was set up by the bed.

Wanting to be certain the police could leave word, Andy turned it on.

/ By the time they reached the party Andy felt better. It helped being met at the door by loud music, bright lights, and a crowd that spilled onto the front steps. People were glad to see them.

"Is Beth Ann going to be here?" he asked Paul as they worked their way through the crowd.

"Didn't know you were interested in her."

"I need something," Andy said.

In the packed kitchen they found cans of soda in a tub of ice. "What's up?" Paul asked a friend.

"Beer's out back," came the answer. Paul ducked out immediately.

Andy felt a tap on his shoulder. It was Sally, a girl from his high school.

"Come on and dance," she said. "There's no

one good here." She pulled Andy into the room where the local garage band was sweating out songs.

Over the din Andy told Sally about the call. "That was cool the way you kept him on," she said. It made him feel good. He tried to decide if he should be interested in her.

/ It was almost one, the time he was due home, when Andy returned to a dark apartment. He hoped his father hadn't fallen asleep; he wanted to be with him, to talk things out as they usually did. Quietly, he called into his father's room. No answer. He went in and noticed that the red light on the answering machine was glowing.

Thinking that the police must have called, he quickly checked. There were two messages; one was from his Aunt Mary, his mother's sister, calling to say hello. The second was from his father, explaining he would be home later than expected.

Andy walked into the living room, flicking on lights as he entered. The empty but cluttered apartment made him feel uncomfortable. He heard thunder and, soon, a pattering rain. He listened intently but something was missing.

Then it came to him. In the house where they used to live, the rain beat down on the roof with a steady drum. In the apartment, all he heard was a hiss. It made Andy feel a long way from home.

He wished his father would hurry. . . .

Later, lying in bed, Andy heard the voice of Zeke saying "I just killed someone" as if the phone were right next to his ear.

He shuddered. But at last, with the lights still on, he drifted off to sleep.

/ In his own bed, the man who called himself Zeke also slept.

/ Next morning, it was still raining. As soon as Andy got up, he looked into his father's room. His father was asleep.

From the front steps he retrieved the newspaper, which was wrapped in plastic, and went through the pages carefully. There was nothing about a murder.

/ " 'Morning," his father said when he came into the kitchen.

Dr. Zadinski was taller than Andy, over-weight and balding. There was a time when he joked with people, told bad puns. But a year ago Andy's mother died, and the jokes died with her. Andy worried about his father.

"Sorry I got in so late," he said. "How was your party?"

"Okay," Andy said. "How was yours?"

"Once I got there, good. The Fillmores are nice. They asked about you." He started to make coffee. "We going to put things away today?"

"Sure."

Dr. Zadinski looked out the window. The rain was streaming down. "You know, your mother actually liked this kind of day."

The memory brought silence.

Andy said, "Aunt Mary called."

"What did she say?"

"Just a message that she called."

"I'll give her a ring."

Andy watched his father staring out the window and wondered if it was the best time to talk about the call. Only when his father turned to attend the hissing kettle did he say, "Want to hear something weird?"

"All right."

Andy told him about Zeke.

His father listened, poured himself a second

cup of coffee, stirred it, sipped at it cautiously. Then he said, "Sounds like a sick joke."

"I believed it."

"Anything in the paper?"

"Nothing," said Andy. "Probably didn't find her yet."

"Must have been a joke, Andy. Give you odds, the guy's name was fake. Same for the girl's."

"Think so?"

"Why would he phone here?"

"Said he just dialed. Maybe he got your number from the college."

Dr. Zadinski thought it through out loud. "Let's see. Our phone was put in Thursday, right? And that's when we got the number. Okay, Friday, yesterday, my department had an emergency meeting. I took the new number with me. Wrote it on a slip of paper, which I intended to give to the secretary. But I was late for the meeting, and, you know me, I was rushing and forgot to give it to her. Then the meeting went on much longer than expected. Big hassle about basic math. Went until six. Thank God for Phil Lucas. Would have gone on forever without him. Anyway, they'd already locked up the building for the weekend. That's how late it was. I flew out of the place. You know, the Fillmores are an hour's drive. That's why

I got back so late. Anyway, I left the numbe
on the secretary's desk. She was long gone. Ther
I remembered I hadn't even put my name or
it. So, no, it hasn't been listed anywhere. Forge
that."

"Our old number," Andy said suddenly. He
sprang up and punched it in. After three ring:
a robot voice came on: "This number is n
longer in service. This number is no longer ir
service."

Andy hung up, disappointed. "Didn't ever
give the new number."

"Too soon," his father said. "They will. Look
the odds for this guy randomly dialing a phone
and getting us is small. Not probable—but, with
only three exchanges in town, possible. Wha
did the police tell Paul? 'Friday night, full moon,
and welfare checks.' An unpleasant remark
but . . . I'd say, forget about the whole thing."

"It made me sick."

"I don't wonder. How are you doing now?"

"Fine."

Andy put his dirty dishes into the sink, then
reached again for the phone. His father looked
up from the paper. "I bet," Andy said, punch-
ing in the police number, "the cops just forgot
about me."

"Officer Martins," he heard. "May I be of assistance?"

Andy repeated his story, adding that he had called the night before to give the same information. "I was wondering," he said, "what you found out."

"Hold on," said the policeman. "I'll look."

Dr. Zadinski watched Andy. "What's he saying?" he asked.

"He's checking."

"Be careful. They'll think you made the call up."

"Come on!"

"I mean it."

The policeman returned. "Andrew?"

"Yes, sir."

"No reports of homicides last night. No missing persons reported. Nothing that matches your information. Quite a peaceful night in fact."

"Sir," said Andy, "did I do the right thing, talking to the guy, calling you, all that?"

"Absolutely," said the policeman. "Most people would have just hung up. No, even if it was a sick joke—and I'm sure it was—you did the right thing. You never know for sure. But you can put this one out of mind. It was nothing."

Andy hung up. "He says it was a joke."

"Wouldn't want it to be true, would you?"

"Are you kidding?" said Andy.

"Tell you what," his father said as he dumped his own dishes into the sink. "Let's get everything put away today. Fast. Then we'll eat out and take in a movie. And tomorrow . . ." Stopping midsentence, he turned away.

"What?" said Andy.

"Andy . . . I've been thinking. . . ."

Puzzled, Andy waited for him to go on.

"Look," his father said finally, still not looking at Andy. "I don't think we should go to the cemetery tomorrow. I know it's a year, or close to it. . . . And we've been planning to go. I bet that's why your Aunt Mary called last night. But you know as well as I do, we keep putting it off. First bad weather. Selling the house. Then moving in here. I don't think either of us wants to go. Am I right?" He turned to look at Andy.

Andy didn't know what he thought.

"It's time to stop," his father said softly.

"Stop what?"

His father made a vague gesture. "Feeling bad. Mourning. Andy, we loved her. We still do. Always will. But . . ." His voice broke. "It's time to let it go. Look," he said, his voice stronger, "if the weather's nice tomorrow, let's do something fun. What do you say?"

"You decide," said Andy.

"No cemetery."

/ When Andy and his father came in that night, the answering machine light was on. Once again Andy thought it was the police. Once again he was wrong. The message was an invitation for Sunday afternoon at the home of one of his father's friends.

"What do you say?" Dr. Zadinski asked.

Andy could tell what his father wanted by his expression. "Suits me," said Andy.

/ At the gathering on Sunday Andy stood around, feeling bored and out of place. Most of the guests were from the college, people he knew only vaguely. Then the host told him there was a real arcade video game in the basement. Andy was welcome to play it as much as he liked.

Later on other kids his age showed up. They made the party better. As for his father, Andy noted he spent most of his time talking to some woman Andy didn't know. And laughing.

/ Monday morning in school, between classes, he was walking down the hallway when Paul ran into him. "Hear anything?" Paul asked.

"What about?"

"That call."

Andy shook his head.

"Told you," Paul said, giving Andy a thumbs-up sign before disappearing into the crowd.

Andy remained where he was. He could hear Zeke saying "I just killed someone" again and again, and wished Paul hadn't reminded him. He didn't want to remember.

/ Once classes were over, he biked to the college to get his father's college library card. The book collection there was huge, and much better than the high school library's for doing research. Andy wanted to get started early on a term paper.

Madison State College, with its seven thousand students and mostly new red brick buildings, was like a second home to him. He knew the whole campus, from the basketball courts to the Old Chapel. For as long as he could remember his father had taught in the Mathematics Department, and used a small, windowless, book-filled office on the third floor of Brazell Hall.

The door was open but his father was out. A fast check of the posted schedule told Andy that his father was still in class. Willing to wait, Andy pulled a book from his bag and settled down in the easy chair Dr. Zadinski kept for students.

The desk phone rang.

Andy hesitated, then decided there was no reason not to answer. "Hello?" he said.

"Robert?" came the voice. It was a woman.

"He's teaching," said Andy. "Can I take a message?"

"That's all right. I'll call back." The woman hung up.

Andy did the same. But instead of returning to the easy chair he sat at the desk, his attention caught by the college phone book. The sight of it brought to mind something Zeke had said, that the girl—Nina Klemmer—went to the college. Andy also remembered his father saying the name was probably false. Though he felt slightly foolish, Andy knew he'd feel better if he checked and saw for himself that the name wasn't there.

He flipped through the pages. On page 62, he saw:

Nina Klemmer . . . . Whig Hall 2409

For a long time he stared at the name. "Not possible," he said to himself, wanting no real name connected to Zeke.

He reached for the phone and dialed the number. Just as quickly he put the receiver down, not sure what he was trying to do.

But Andy stayed by the desk, wondering if the Nina Klemmer in the book was the one Zeke had spoken about, wondering if she had been killed.

He dialed again. This time, when the phone started ringing, he held on.

"Whig Third!" a woman announced.

Andy cleared his throat. "Is . . . is Nina Klemmer there?" he said. It felt odd to speak her name.

"Nina?"

"Right. Nina."

"Hang on. I think I just saw her going to her library job." The phone clattered down.

Puzzled and nervous, Andy waited.

"Hello!" The voice rang out with a breathy, brassy energy.

"Is . . . is this Nina Klemmer?" Andy asked.

"Sure is."

"My name is Andrew . . . Andy Zadinski, and I . . ."

"Yes?"

"I was calling . . . to tell you something."

"What's that?"

"See," Andy tried, "I live in town. I don't go here. But my father is in the Math Department. In the college . . . and . . ."

"What's this have to do with me?"

"What I'm trying to say . . . Look," Andy stumbled on, attempting a different tack, "I don't want to scare you or anything . . ."

"Why should I be scared? Would you just tell me why you're calling? I've got to go to the library."

"Did the police call you?" Andy blurted out.

"No, the police didn't call me and I don't like oddball calls from guys I don't know."

"I *do* know you!"

"Really," she said, and hung up.

Now feeling he *must* explain, Andy dialed again. Nina picked up on the first ring. "Hey, man, stop pestering me," she said right off. "Else I'll call the cops." She hung up.

Nina Klemmer was not dead. Andy felt like an idiot.

/ "Hello," his father said, walking into the office with a student. "This is a surprise."

Agitated, disappointed that his father wasn't alone, that they couldn't talk, Andy said, "Can I borrow your college library card? I have a paper to do."

"No problem." His father dug into his wallet. As he handed the card over he looked carefully at his son. "Something up?" he asked.

Andy, with a glance at the student, shook his head. "Tell you later."

His father gave a nod of understanding. "Dinner by seven?" he asked.

"Okay."

"Whose turn to cook?"

"Yours."

"Right-o. See you then."

Andy remembered the message he'd taken. "Someone called. A woman. Said she'd call back."

/In front of the library stood a tulip tree, its pink flowers filling the air with a sweet assurance that spring had come. Students sat around it, soaking up the sun. They seemed so sophisticated to Andy, so much at ease, and they made him wonder what he'd be like when he reached college. He assumed he would go, but he had no idea where. Sometimes he thought it would be Madison State. At other times he considered places far away. Andy liked thinking about the future. The past was something he tried to avoid. The past meant death.

He had known—for as long as he could remember—that his parents named him after his father's brother, who had died suddenly in his sleep when still a young man. And his earliest distinct memory was of a midsummer morning when their family dog was killed. She lay in a cardboard box, black curly hair blotched with blood. When Andy's mother tried to explain what had happened—that part Andy didn't recall—she wept. He had never seen his mother cry before.

Two of his grandparents had died—one of them of a long, lingering illness—in nursing homes. The other suffered a series of strokes.

Andy had seen that grandfather strapped to a chair so he wouldn't fall out and hurt himself. Spit dribbled over his slack lips, down his unshaven, toothless chin. He had no idea who Andy was. Yet it was he who had taught Andy to bait a hook, to throw a curve, to ride a bike.

A year ago Andy's mother had been killed by a drunken driver who hit her car. That morning she had given Andy breakfast—juice, French toast, and milk—kissed him good-bye, and reminded him of a dentist appointment at four. He never saw her again, dead or alive.

His father, the police, even Paul had said the phone call was a joke. To Andy, talk of death was never—ever—a joke.

In his usual corner at the top of the library, a partially hidden lounge chair by a window that overlooked trees and a parking lot, Andy tried to think about his paper, tried to read. But thoughts of Nina Klemmer kept filling his mind: *She is real. And alive.* She said the police hadn't called her.

Didn't she need to know that someone talked of killing her?

As a way of not thinking about the answer,

he made himself concentrate on the economic reasons for the American Civil War.

/A loudspeaker in the ceiling blared, "Would Mr. Matthews please come to the Circulation Desk."

Andy leaned back in his chair and stared at the speaker. He had never noticed it before. . . . An idea struck him.

When he had called Nina Klemmer, the person who answered told him Nina was about to leave for her library job. Nina said so herself. She was probably in the building, right then.

Andy tried to think it through: Nina Klemmer's name was real. Zeke had not made that up. Still, he might have picked the name at random. "Not probable, but possible," as his father would say.

Andy recalled Zeke's description of her, how precise it was. If he, Andy, could see her, if she bore *no* resemblance to Zeke's description, it would prove Zeke had picked her name at random, just as he had picked their phone number at random. Therefore—Andy was trying to think logically—if Nina Klemmer looked different than Zeke had said, it would prove the call a joke. And if it were a joke, Andy would be able to put the business out of his mind.

Gathering his books, he returned quickly to the library lobby, a wide, open space with a threadbare red carpet. At the entrance, thirty feet from the long checkout counter, were turnstiles and, nearby, phone booths. Andy went to one. When he looked up Madison State College in the phone book he found the library's number.

Andy dialed it.

"Madison State College Library," he heard.

"Can you help me," said Andy, edging out of the booth to watch the lobby counter. A young library clerk held a phone to his ear. "I'll try," Andy heard and watched the clerk say.

"There's someone named Nina Klemmer in the library," he told the clerk. "I need to speak to her. It's an emergency. Can you page her?"

"We don't like to do that," the young man said. "Not if it's an ordinary matter."

"Honest," said Andy. "It is an emergency. Nina Klemmer."

"Hold on, please," the young man said, and moved along the counter where he picked up a microphone. At once, his voice blared over the public address system. "Would Nina Klemmer please come to the Circulation Desk."

Andy slipped back into the phone booth and let the receiver dangle on its cord, then stepped out and waited. In moments a young woman appeared.

She was tall, thin, and wore baggy clothes. But there was nothing sloppy about her. The colors she wore were bold . . . reds, blacks, and yellows. Her high-heeled boots, turned down at the tops, were white. Her hair was black, cropped short, and seemed to shimmer. Around her wrists she wore glittering bracelets. Her fingernails were scarlet. Her face, highlighted with bright red lipstick and darkly lined eyes, was pale, almost white, with high cheekbones that made Andy think of a fashion model's. Not only was she stunning to look at, she fit Zeke's description.

At the counter Nina Klemmer spoke to the clerk, who handed her the phone. From his place across the lobby Andy could see her mouth the word "Hello?" twice. When she received no answer, she asked the clerk something and offered the phone to him. The clerk listened, then shrugged and hung up. Nina Klemmer faced the lobby, a frown on her face. Then she moved quickly away.

Snatching up his books, Andy followed.

/ She went down a corridor and pushed through some double doors. When Andy reached the same spot he heard her heels clicking down to a lower level. He kept on after her.

On the lower level, she made a left, went up a hallway ramp, and took a sharp right through yet another pair of doors. Andy's heart was pounding.

She went by some study desks and made still another turn. Following quickly, Andy came to the place where magazines were given out. He stopped. There she was, behind a counter, talking to another student.

Surprised to have come upon her so abruptly, Andy stopped short. "Looking for something?" the other student asked.

Andy attempted to cover his confusion by saying, "This where you get the magazines?"

"Fill out a call slip and we'll get you what you want." The student held out a bit of yellow paper. "Have you checked to see what you need?"

Andy took the paper. "Where do I do that?" he said. He was afraid to look at Nina.

"Upstairs."

Andy fled.

Secure in his top-floor place, he tried to grasp what he had just learned.

Nina Klemmer looked *exactly* the way Zeke had described her. So he had *not* picked her name at random. She was someone he had watched with care.

"He's going to kill her," Andy said to himself.

Part Two

On the way back to the apartment, Andy biked past the school ball field. When he saw a pickup game in progress and Paul at bat, he stopped. Paul spotted him.

"Come on and play!" he called.

"Don't have my glove," said Andy.

"You can use mine."

"Or mine," someone else said.

"Come on!" Paul called again.

Andy propped his bike against the batting cage and with a borrowed mitt on his hand took the field. Paul's first hit, a sharp chopper to the left, drove thoughts of Nina out of Andy's mind.

/ "Hi!" his father called from the kitchen when Andy came in. "Get your work done?"

"I was playing ball," Andy answered, then dumped his books in his room before coming back to set the table.

His father said, "You'll never guess what happened to me today."

"What?"

"Guess."

Andy caught something different in his father's voice and looked over at him. Dr. Zadinski was grinning broadly. "I don't know," Andy said.

"I've got a date."

"What do you mean?"

His father's look of pleasure faded. "A date," he repeated. "Me. I'm going out with someone on Friday."

"You mean . . . a woman?"

"She's not exactly a poodle."

"No kidding. Who?"

"Remember yesterday, I met this woman?"

Andy tried to recall but couldn't.

"She called me. Suggested we go to a movie."

"She called you just like that?"

"Hey, new age. Not bad, eh?" His father was grinning broadly again.

It pleased Andy to see him cheerful. He smiled too. "What's her name?"

"Peggy. Peggy Anderson. She's in the Special Ed. Department."

"Great."

"Actually," his father said, "I'm nervous. Been a long time since I went on a date. Ever get nervous when you date?"

"We don't date."

"Right, and I'm too old to hang out at the Mall." He gave Andy a questioning look. "It . . . doesn't bother you, does it?" he asked. Their eyes met.

"What?"

"Me . . . going out?"

At the question Andy realized it did bother him. But when he looked at his father and saw him smiling in a way he hadn't seen for a long time, he said, "Hey, it's good for you."

Dr. Zadinski brought dinner to the table. "How come you played ball?" he asked. "I thought you were going to the library."

"Something happened."

"Spring fever?"

"Really want to know?"

"Always."

Andy pushed himself away from the table and went into his father's room to find the college phone book. He brought it back, laid it in front of his father, opened it to the right page, and pointed out Nina's name.

"I don't understand," his father said.

"That call," said Andy. "Friday. Remember? You said it was a phony name. Well, it isn't. Look." He jabbed the page. Then he told his father what he had done, all of it, including paging Nina Klemmer in the library. When he was finished, he said, "Still think it was a gag?"

"Yes. And I don't think it was so great using the library's emergency system like that."

"Dad, he described her, just the way she is! And he said he killed her. That's more than a joke, isn't it? I mean, shouldn't she know what's going on?"

His father shook his head. "You gave the police a full report. Twice. They can decide what to do."

"She said they didn't tell her."

"So what? It's most likely what the cop said. Nothing. Which is why they didn't. Eat your dinner before it gets cold."

"It's not wrong, is it, to tell someone she's in danger?"

"Andy, it's *you* who think she's in danger. I mean, she's probably used to that kind of thing. You said she was pretty."

"Are you serious?"

"Look, you asked for my advice. The cops are pros. They know what to do. You don't. Some sick guy, you haven't the foggiest notion who, gets off on—"

The phone rang, making them both jump. It was one of Dr. Zadinski's colleagues. Andy waited for him to hang up so they could finish the conversation, but when the call stretched on with no break in sight Andy finished eating, cleaned up, and went into his room. By then he had decided his father really didn't want to talk about it. And there was homework to do.

/ Later that night his father came into Andy's room. "What's a good place to eat out?" he asked.

"For what?"

"My date."

"The Lobster Place," said Andy, suggesting the fanciest restaurant he knew.

"Good idea. 'Night, kid. See you in the morning."

"Dad?"

"What's that?"

"Maybe the police just forgot to check the college about Nina Klemmer?" His father gave him a blank look. "The call . . . ," Andy reminded him.

"Andy, three things. Leave it alone. Forget it. And get some sleep. It's late."

Andy undressed slowly for bed, as always flinging his dirty clothes toward the hamper in the closet and missing.

He thought about his father's date and wondered if he would marry the woman—what was her name? He pushed the thought aside; after all, his father had only just met her.

He thought about Nina Klemmer. Perhaps the police didn't call the college because—like his father until Andy told him the truth—they didn't believe she was real.

Andy got into bed, deciding he'd feel better if he let the police know what he'd discovered. After all, he reminded himself, the police told him he had done the right thing when he called the first time. Why not a second time?

/When school was over on Tuesday Andy and Paul left the building together. Paul said, "You hear? They announced baseball tryouts for next week. You're going out for it, aren't you?"

"I might," Andy said, although he knew he would.

"Mr. Howells thinks you're good."

"How do you know?"

"He was talking to a bunch of us about guys he hoped would come out for the team. He mentioned you."

"He did?" Andy said, pleased.

"Tony was there," Paul said. "Ask him. You'd be crazy not to try out."

"Probably will," Andy said, keeping cool, but wondering which position Mr. Howells wanted him to play.

In the bright sunlight buses were taking on students. Kids were milling about, shouting, laughing, reluctant to leave.

"Hey," Paul said. "Let's play this afternoon. We can get some guys. Hey, Brad," he said, grabbing a boy who was passing. "Want to play ball?"

"Sure, when?"

"At the field. Tell the others."

Brad went off.

Andy looked at his watch. "How long you going to play?"

"I don't know. Till around five. Why?"

"Got to do something first," Andy said. "Then I'll come over."

/The Madison Municipal Building, three quarters of a mile from the school, housed most of the town offices, including the Police Department. At the entrance to the police section, a white-haired policeman was sitting behind a desk marked INFORMATION.

"Help you, kid?" he said, as Andy approached.

Andy explained, "I need to speak to someone."

"A complaint? A fine? A license?"

"I found out something else about a crime I reported."

The policeman's eyebrows went up. "A crime you committed?"

"I reported it," Andy said again. "May I talk to someone in charge?"

"I am talking to you," the policeman said. All the same he reached for his desk phone and dialed a number. "Front desk here," he said. "Kid here wants to talk to someone about a crime he says he reported. Says he has more information. Maybe you can see him for a few minutes, okay?"

"Officer Dorfman," the policeman told Andy, holding out a card. "Room 65. Through those doors. Show that pass."

The young policeman behind the desk in Room 65 looked up.

"Are you Officer Dorfman?" Andy asked.

"That's me," said the policeman and waved Andy toward a seat. "Want to give me your name?"

Andy sat down. "Andy," he said. "Andy Zadinski."

"Okay, Andy, what can I do for you?"

Andy told his story while from time to time Dorfman took notes.

"I thought you might not have checked the college," Andy concluded. "I mean, this guy, whoever he is, must be watching her. I think she should be warned."

Dorfman said nothing. Instead, he studied Andy silently, then tilted his swivel chair back, one shoe against the top edge of his desk, hands behind his head. "Okay," he said at last. "Basically, you did the right thing by calling us when the guy called you. I wish everyone was as responsible."

Andy was glad he'd come.

"Second," continued Dorfman, "I can understand your curiosity about what might have happened when you called us the next day. Only human nature. But I have to believe what you were told was correct: Nothing happened."

"Except—"

"Let me finish," said Dorfman. "Finally, I can see you checking out this girl's name in that college phone book. Again, good thinking. As for the rest, no way. Leave it alone."

"But . . ."

"Andy, let me ask you some questions, okay?"

"Yes, sir."

Dorfman leaned over the desk toward him. "Could the person who called you, this Zeke, be a friend of yours? You know, someone out for a laugh?"

"We only got the phone the day before," Andy explained. "No one had the number except Paul."

"Paul?"

"I told you. My best friend. He'd just come over."

"When did he get it?"

"Just then. I wrote it down for him."

Dorfman pursed his lips. "How about this. . . . While you were doing something . . . in the can, say . . . this Paul calls another buddy and sets you up. Suckers you."

Andy shook his head. "We were together all the time. Besides, he's not that way. I told you, we're best friends. And anyway he didn't know the number before the guy called."

"Okay," continued Dorfman, smiling. "But still, basically, that guy was making a bad joke."

"But he *described* her," said Andy. "*Exactly*. Which means he's been watching her. It has to be real."

"Andy, listen up. *Is* she dead?"

"No . . ."

"Then what he said *wasn't* real, was it?"

Andy blushed, but persisted. "Aren't you even going to warn her?" he said.

Dorfman picked up a pencil and tapped it against a fingernail a few times. "Andy," he said, "I assume the Madison Police Department has taken care of the matter properly."

"I know, but . . ."

Dorfman gave a forced smile. "Tell you what I'll do. Soon as you leave, I'll check this out and make sure everything that should have been done was done. Fair enough?"

"Will you tell her?" Andy asked. "And me?"

Dorfman shook his head. "You've done your part. Leave the rest to us."

Andy sat there not knowing what to do or say to convince Dorfman to be serious. The call *was* about killing. After a moment the police-man said, "That's it, my friend. I've work to do. Thanks for coming."

Reluctantly, Andy got up and started to go. Just as he reached the door, Dorfman stopped him.

Andy turned back.

"Andy, did anyone, other than you, I mean, actually *hear* this guy?"

"No," Andy said, puzzled by the question.

"So you're the only proof we've got that he called?"

"Well, yes . . ."

"Let me ask you: You ever see or hear about this girl before? You said she was a looker."

"I don't understand."

"Andy," said Dorfman, "this isn't some joke of *yours*, is it? A way to meet the girl? Impress her? Get on her good side. Something like that."

Andy was shocked. "Oh, no, I'm not—"

Dorfman cut him off. "Okay, pal," he said, sounding amused. "Just checking out all pos-sibilities." He waved Andy away.

/As Andy went home he de-cided not to tell his father what had happened at the police station. He was in no mood to hear

"I told you so," or be reminded of his father's advice to forget it.

Once he got to the apartment he remembered about playing ball with Paul and the other guys. But by then it was too late, and in any case, he'd lost his energy. As far as Andy was concerned the afternoon had been a waste.

And by Wednesday morning he'd made up his mind to trash the whole business. His father was right, there was nothing he could do about Nina Klemmer. The police could handle it. He was going to trust them.

That afternoon he played ball. When practice was over he felt his swing was getting into a decent groove. It was his fielding he had to work on, learning to keep his head down, his eyes on the ball when it came right at him. He tended to duck, back off. The only way was to charge every shot. Take command. Coach Howells had told him that again and again the year before. It was still true.

/ "Good afternoon, Andy. I'm glad we found you," Mrs. Baskin said when he entered the school counselor's office. "We need to talk, you and I."

Andy sat down. That morning he had been

given a message that she wanted to see him eighth period. He had no idea why.

"How have you been?" she asked.

"Fine."

"Things sorting out?"

"Sure."

Each time Andy answered, Mrs. Baskin allowed a space of silence. Not knowing what to do with the space, Andy began to feel on edge.

"I see," she said, "that you and your father moved into town, closer to school, and to your friend Paul," she added with a smile. "Moving can be very upsetting, especially if it's from a home you love, where you grew up. How do you feel about it?"

"Okay," said Andy, still puzzled about why she had called him.

Mrs. Baskin opened a folder that lay on her desk, read the top page, then put it aside. "Andy," she said, her eyes steadily on him, "I received a call from the town police . . . an Officer Dorfman."

Andy sat bolt upright. "Dorfman?"

"He wanted to know something about your background. I gather you were involved in . . . what shall I say . . . an obscene phone call."

"The guy called *me!*" Andy cried.

"Tell me," suggested Mrs. Baskin.

Exasperated, Andy explained about the call as well as his efforts to get someone to warn Nina Klemmer. "That's why I went to the police," he said. "I was trying to help her. He didn't believe me, did he?" He dropped back against the chair.

Mrs. Baskin said, "Andy, do you know the story about the boy who cried 'Wolf!' Remember? A sheepherder, a boy like you, was very lonely and wanted company, people to pay attention to him. So he called for help when no wolf was there. People came running but they found nothing. Then, when a wolf truly did come, and the boy cried out for help, no one came. And the sheep and the boy . . . perished."

"It's not like that," Andy told her.

"Andy," she said softly, "just about a year ago your mother was killed."

"What's that have to do with it?"

"Remember we talked about what you were feeling then? And about the future?"

Andy nodded, looked away.

"When these . . . sad, tragic, painful anniversaries occur, it's normal, and reasonable, that a person thinks about what happened. He begins to live through those awful moments again, to do things—"

"I didn't do anything," Andy insisted.

"You did speak to that college student. You went to the police. That's something."

"I'm worried about her."

"But if the call was a joke . . ."

"It was real!" Andy cried.

Mrs. Baskin looked at him thoughtfully. "What does your father say about all this?"

"He says I should leave it alone."

"Sometimes, Andy," said Mrs. Baskin, her voice hushed, "it takes a long, long time for people to show their grief. Do you think it's possible that only now you're feeling the loss of someone who loved you very much, whom you loved?"

Andy showed his disgust with silence.

"Let me tell you something about people who are upset," she continued. "When they hide from what's hurting them, from reality, it only makes them more upset. Face reality and things become clear. Now, I'd like to talk about this again, next week, when you've had time to think about that."

Andy pulled himself forward in his chair. "I'd like to know something," he said.

"Certainly."

"Do *you* think I made up that call, that I'm hiding from . . . what did you say . . . reality?"

"My honest answer is . . . I don't know," she said, smiling. "Now, we can met again Monday, eighth period. I've checked your schedule. You've got a study hall then. Let's make it a whole period."

"Do I have a choice?" asked Andy.

Mrs. Baskin smiled again. "I think not," she said.

/ Andy stood in the hallway outside Mrs. Baskin's office, furious at both her and Dorfman.

"You okay?"

Andy looked up. It was Sally. She was wearing a coat that was much too big for her.

Andy made a motion toward Mrs. Baskin's office door. "Remember that call I got? That weirdo I told you about?"

She nodded yes.

"They think I made it up."

"You're kidding."

"Because a year ago my mother got killed."

"I don't get it," said Sally.

"Neither do I. But now she wants to see me every week."

"Will you?"

Andy shrugged. "I don't know."

"There's a bunch of people going over to McDonald's. It's Sue's birthday. Want to come?"

"I'm in no mood."

"Come on," she said, taking him by the arm. "It'll make you feel better."

When they got to the restaurant ten kids were already there. One of them had arranged a McDonald's party for Sue, who was just sixteen—a party complete with balloons, party favors, and someone dressed up like Ronald McDonald. Andy tried to enjoy the fooling around but couldn't get into it. He kept thinking about Mrs. Baskin's story, about the boy who cried "Wolf!" As he saw it, his situation was just the opposite. He *was* crying, but about a *real* wolf. It was other people who were refusing to believe the truth: Nina Klemmer needed to be warned. Her life was in danger but he was the only one willing to take the fact seriously.

At dinner that evening, Andy told his father about Mrs. Baskin.

"How did she find out about the call?" he wanted to know.

Surprised by the question, Andy tried to duck it with a shrug.

"You tell people at school?" his father pressed.

"I guess."

"I warned you. People grab on to what they hear, especially if there's some mystery involved."

"It's just wrong," Andy said, pushing his plate away.

"What are you going to do," his father inquired, "set the world right by yourself? Go and see Mrs. Baskin a couple of times. It won't hurt. Want me to call her?"

"No," Andy said, worried what his father might say if he learned he'd gone to the police.

Dr. Zadinski sighed. "It'll blow over." He studied Andy carefully. "*Are* you upset about it . . . being a year ago? Or the move? Would you like me to cancel my date?"

"What date?"

"Tomorrow, with Peggy . . ."

"I don't want to talk about it," said Andy, wishing people would stick to the point. "Where you going with her?"

"You suggested it," his father replied with a smile. "The Lobster Place."

"You driving to where she lives, picking her up, paying for dinner . . . the whole fifties bit?"

The color drained from Dr. Zadinski's face.

"What's the matter?"

"I forgot to work that out," his father said. He got up and headed for the bedroom phone.

"She probably didn't bring that up on purpose," Andy called after him. "She *wanted* you to call her."

His father came back with a shy smile. "Think so?"

"Sure. She likes you."

Andy finished eating and cleaning up, then stole a look into his father's room. He was on his bed, shoes kicked off, tie loosened, sitting propped up against a pillow. After forty-five minutes of talking the phone was still stuck to his ear. Andy could see he was having a good time.

"I'm going for a walk," Andy let him know.

Dr. Zadinski waved in response.

Hands in pockets, Andy started walking with no particular direction in mind but before he realized it, he was halfway to the college.

By day the campus of Madison State was like a park with carefully groomed lawns and trees. By night the greens turned dark, and the empty classroom buildings became ghostly hulks. Walkway lamps cast feeble pools of light, and people moved with hurried steps.

Yet the campus was open. No fence or guards

blocked entry. People could and did enter at will. Andy had done so countless times, meeting his father or coming to watch a sporting event.

That night the stars were out. The air was soft and balmy. Couples sat on lawns. From an open dorm window, music pulsed. Except for the library, whose lights blazed, the main buildings lay in shadow. Andy headed there.

Knowing that Nina had no idea what he looked like, Andy openly searched the building's three floors before getting the nerve to go to the magazine section where he had seen her before.

"Is Nina Klemmer around?" he asked.

"She just left."

"Know where?"

The student, a girl, considered Andy. "You her friend?"

"Yeah."

"Probably went to her dorm. Or the Student Center."

Andy didn't see her at first.

He checked the eating area. It was served by a snack bar and was built on a lower level than the two-story, tree-filled atrium. Though it had many tables and eating booths, Andy could survey the entire space from the top of the steps. He spotted her sitting alone in a back booth, sipping a can of soda and reading an open notebook. She was dressed in a black jump suit, a white sash around her waist, and another white band over her hair. Her lipstick was purple, her dangling plastic earrings, blue.

Andy walked toward her but stopped a few feet away, hoping she would look up. She remained intent on her reading.

He moved closer to her booth but still she didn't notice. "Nina . . . ," he said.

Nina jerked her head up.

"Can . . . I . . . can I talk to you?"

Puzzled, Nina stared at him. "What?" she said.

"I need to talk to you."

"What about?"

"It's important."

"Who are you?" she asked.

"Andy. Andy Zadinski," he said, slipping into the opposite booth bench.

When he sat Nina stiffened, ready to bolt. "What do you want?" she said.

"Look . . . ," said Andy. "Last week . . . Friday . . . at my home . . . this guy called me. Said his name was Zeke. I mean, I don't know who he is. And he . . . ." Andy stopped when Nina flipped her notebook shut. "See," he went on, "this guy started to talk about you."

"Me?"

"Right. Described you. *Exactly*. The way you are."

Nina cocked her head. "This for real?"

"Honest. It's what happened."

Nina considered Andy carefully, then suddenly stood up. "I'm not interested."

Andy impulsively grabbed her wrist to keep her from leaving. "He said he killed you."

Nina freed herself with a yank of her arm, then stopped, open-mouthed, staring at Andy, her face paler than before. She rubbed the place where he had held her. It was a little red. "He said *what*?" she whispered.

Andy dropped his voice. "That he . . . killed you."

"Are you out of your mind?" Nina said, looking around to see if anyone else was near.

Andy rushed on. "See, there was this friend of mine with me, Paul. I told him to get the police and trace the call while I talked to Zeke. But they couldn't. You can't do that easily except on TV. Then, you know, *I* called the police to tell them. Even went to the station. But they said, 'Forget it. It was a gag. A joke.' See?"

"He said he was going to *kill* me?" Nina repeated.

"No, he said he *had* killed you. And he described you, too. You know, the way you look and dress. That you're, you know, good-looking. Everything."

"But . . . *who*?"

"Right. That's the whole point. He said his name was Zeke. But I don't know. I mean, I told the whole thing to the police so they could warn you. But they didn't, did they?"

Nina shook her head.

"That's what I was afraid of," Andy said. "I thought you should know."

"Monday." Nina suddenly said. "Monday afternoon. Did you call me?"

"I wanted to tell you . . ."

"And a little later, page me in the library . . ."

"So I could see if you fit Zeke's description."

"Look, kid, I don't know who you are or what you want, but . . . You a student here?"

"I go to high school in—"

Nina cut him off. "You've got no right to do this to me or even be here. I mean, you better clear out or I'll—"

"No, look . . . ," tried Andy.

Nina wouldn't let him speak. "Zeke, or Andy, or whatever your name is, so help me, I'm going to report this. And if you ever bother me again . . ." She didn't finish but hurried away, almost running out of the area. People twisted in their seats to look at her, then at Andy.

Andy was stunned.

/ When he arrived home his father was in the living room, reading. "I was getting worried," he said, putting the book aside. "Where you been?"

Andy didn't know how to start. He sat down and looked at his hands.

"Andy?" his father asked. "What's the matter?"

"Wait a minute. I'll tell you." Andy pressed his hands together tightly to control his nervousness but still couldn't make himself look up. Finally he said, "I don't understand this. I don't."

"What are you talking about?"

"That call," Andy explained. "Zeke saying he was going to kill . . . had killed her."

"Zeke?"

"That call. Last Friday."

His father made the connection. "What's happened now?"

Andy forced himself to look up. "When I went to the police—"

"Police?" his father cut in. "When did you go to them? And why?"

"Two days ago. To tell them that there really is a Nina Klemmer. That Zeke is watching her. That she's in danger. Only, the cop I spoke to didn't believe me. All he did was call Mrs. Baskin, the counselor at my school."

"You told me . . ."

"The cop thought it was me trying to get attention from this Nina."

"Andy . . ."

"Dad, she needs to know. From what Mrs. Baskin said I know they won't tell her. So, just now, I went over to the college to find her myself."

"And . . . ?"

"In the Student Center . . . I tried to talk to her. That's *all*."

"What happened?"

"She got it all wrong. Thought I was . . . bothering . . . pestering her. Said she was going to report me to the police." Andy looked directly at his father. "Why doesn't anybody believe me?"

"That it?"

"Yeah."

"No more?"

Andy shook his head.

"You give her your name?" his father asked.

"Sure."

Dr. Zadinski sighed. "Andy, the college is very concerned about harassment. Kids call in bomb threats during exam periods. Lots of false alarms. Women have been assaulted. Mugged."

"That's nothing to do with me," Andy said.

For a while neither of them spoke. Then Dr. Zadinski drew himself up. "Okay," he said. "I'm going to ask you something and you *must* give me an absolutely truthful answer. No matter what you say, I'm going to defend you. But understand, I *must* know the truth. A deal?"

"I don't know what you're talking about."

"Am I going to get a straight answer?"

"All right. Yes. What is it?"

"That call," his father began, "the one you said you got . . . Andy, look up at me. Right into my eyes. Did you . . . maybe with Paul's help . . . make up the whole thing?"

"Are you serious?" Andy cried.

"Give me an answer!" his father insisted.

"It was real!" Andy snapped back.

Dr. Zadinski scrutinized his son for a long time. Then he said, "Okay."

"Thanks a bunch."

After a moment his father began to pace the room.

Andy watched. "You work out your date?" he asked.

"My what?"

"Your date. Tomorrow."

"Peggy. Oh, yes, fine. The place you suggested."

"Great."

"I'd better call it off."

"Why?"

"I'm not sure if tomorrow is a good time for me to be out."

"What's that got to do with it?" Andy asked.

"I should be around if something happens."

"What could happen?"

His father spun around. "Did you even *think* of the consequences? What if this girl does file charges?" Andy winced. "No, first thing in the morning, we'd better call the policeman you spoke to. Head him off. And Mrs. Baskin. No. Let's go to your school first. Together. We'll see her, show her I'm behind you, get her on your side. Things might go easier."

Andy felt both grateful and embarrassed. "You don't have to call off your date," he said, sorry he had made problems for his father.

"Let's see what happens," Dr. Zadinski replied.

/ At eight o'clock the next morning Andy and his father walked through the school building toward Mrs. Baskin's office. The halls were already crowded with students, and as they turned down the last hall Andy saw Paul.

Andy reached out to pull his father another way but it was too late. Paul had seen them.

"Hi," he said, coming up to them. "How you doing, Dr. Z? What's happening?" He looked from Andy to Dr. Zadinski.

"Hello, Paul," said Dr. Zadinski. "I'm just meeting with one of the math teachers here. How you been?"

"Fine. I gotta go. Nice to see you." He gave Andy a wink. "Catch you later," he said, and rushed off.

Dr. Zadinski turned toward Andy. "See, not everyone need know." But Andy was sure Paul had seen through his father's lie.

When they reached Mrs. Baskin's office they found Officer Dorfman waiting outside the door. Andy's heart sank.

"Hello, Andrew," Dorfman said. "This your father?" He extended a hand to Dr. Zadinski. "Pleased to meet you, sir. Officer Tim Dorfman. Madison Police Department."

"Dr. Robert Zadinski," Andy's father returned. Andy had rarely heard him use his title.

"Did Mrs. Baskin call you in?" Dorfman asked.

"Not at all," Andy's father said. "This was Andy's idea. He wanted to call you, too." As he spoke he glanced at Andy as if to say, *I know it's not true, but let me do the talking.*

"Did you?" said Dorfman, looking at Andy with a slight smile. "Good idea."

Andy was sure Dorfman didn't believe his father. And he wished they could get out of the hall, where students kept passing and gawking.

They waited in awkward silence. When Mrs. Baskin finally stepped out of her office she was surprised to find the Zadinskis there, but quickly recovered. "Dr. Zadinski," she said, "I'm glad to see you."

"This was Andy's idea," he told her. Andy looked away. "Something happened last night that we thought would be best to discuss with you."

"I'm all for that," Dorfman put in.

Mrs. Baskin looked from Dorfman, to Andy, to Andy's father. She said, "I think we better go into my office."

She sat behind her desk, Dorfman on the right, Andy and his father on the left.

"Andy," his father prompted, "why don't you tell them."

Andy took a breath and, looking only at Mrs. Baskin, related what had happened.

"See," he concluded, "this Nina misunderstood. I was only trying to help her." He stole a glance at Dorfman, but Dorfman revealed nothing of his thoughts.

"Did the young woman call you?" Andy's father asked the policeman.

"We had a different story," Dorfman replied. "The college security coordinator, Sergeant Evans—he's in charge of morals problems—informed us that a complaint was called in against Andy here for harassing Nina Klemmer in the college Student Center last night. She alleges he threatened her, used force . . ."

"I was trying to warn her!" Andy cried.

Dorfman shook his head. "Not her story."

"I haven't the slightest doubt she exaggerated," Dr. Zadinski said. "It's totally unlike Andy. Has anything like this ever happened at school?" he asked Mrs. Baskin.

"I'm not aware of it," she replied.

Andy, feeling it was an evasive answer, shook his head in frustration.

His father turned to Dorfman. "Did she have any witnesses?"

The policeman held up his hands. "I've only got an oral report. Evans usually writes pages. I decided to come here first."

Dr. Zadinski asked, "Will official charges be brought?"

"We'll have to see," said Dorfman. "The first thing is to get to the bottom of this."

Andy's father stood up. "If this is a legal matter, I don't think we wish to talk anymore. We came on our own because Andy felt it would be productive. I agreed. But now . . ." He turned to Mrs. Baskin. "What's your position in this?"

"I'm not sure," she admitted.

"Well then," said Dr. Zadinski, giving Andy a nudge to get up, "until a decision has been made we've got nothing more to say. I suppose I should get a lawyer."

"Certainly your right," agreed Dorfman. He was no longer smiling.

Andy suddenly turned on Dorfman. "Why don't you believe me?" he demanded.

Dorfman said, "Give me something to believe."

/ Andy stood with his father in the hallway outside Mrs. Baskin's office.

"What did he mean, 'used force'?" Dr. Zadinski asked.

"I was trying to explain but she jumped up and started to go," said Andy. "I just reached out, you know, no big deal, grabbed her arm, trying to get her to listen."

Andy's father frowned. "Okay," he said, "only from now on you have to tell me *everything*. I can't help with things if I don't know about them."

"Sorry . . ."

"That a deal?"

"Yes," said Andy, feeling that whether he grabbed Nina's arm or not had nothing to do with what was important.

"Where do you want to go?" his father asked him.

"Far away."

"No, I mean, stay in school, go home, or come with me to the college. I've got classes to teach, then a meeting . . ."

"I'll stay here."

His father put a hand behind Andy's neck and gave it a playful shake. "Andy," he said, "remember, when you were a kid, we'd all go out to Hardy Amusement Park."

"What about it?"

"Of all the rides, your favorite was the carousel. You always chose that first. But you had the hardest time deciding which animal to ride. And they had every kind: horses, elephants, dragons. A whole Noah's Ark. Anyway, you'd say you had to pick the one you felt like."

"What's that got to do with anything?"

"We're going to get on our dragons and leave these people in the dust. I know what you did. I know what you didn't do."

"I was trying to warn her."

"Andy . . . you're not going to do any more, right?"

"But, suppose . . ."

"Andy, *nothing*."

Andy turned away.

"And I'll speak to George Perbeck."

"Who's he?"

"A lawyer. He helped when your mother was killed. We can trust him."

Andy began to sense what might happen. "Think she's going to press charges?" he asked.

"We'll have to wait and see."

"If I could only prove . . ."

"Don't even think of it," his father said wearily. He looked at his watch. "I have to go. Whose turn for dinner tonight?"

"You've got a date."

His father blushed at his forgetfulness. "I'll call it off."

"Dad," said Andy, upset that people kept focusing their attention on him, rather than on Nina's danger. Dorfman's remark, "Give me something to believe," particularly rankled. If the police didn't do something, Zeke might act. . . . "Dad, I'm all right."

"Why don't you come back right after school," said his father. "I'll make sure I'm there. We'll talk some more." He made a loose fist and punched Andy on the shoulder. "On your dragon, laddie. Scoot." He started off.

"Don't call off your date," Andy shouted after him.

/ As soon as Andy and Paul met for lunch, Paul demanded, "What's going on?"

"Tell you after we eat."

They went behind the school and sat on the pavement, backs against a wall. Beneath the warm sun Andy told Paul everything that had happened. "The crazy part," he said when he was done, "is that no one believes me."

"Not even your father?"

Andy shook his head.

"How come?"

"I'm not sure. Mrs. Baskin, you know, she told me the story about the boy who cried 'Wolf!' Except, she has it all wrong. There *is* a wolf. You believe it, don't you?"

"Hey, I was there when you got the call."

"I told the cop that," said Andy, "as proof. He said that maybe when I went out of the room you called someone and got him to phone." Andy shook his head at the stupidity.

"Everyone knows about the cop coming to school," said Paul.

Andy picked up a pebble from the ground and flung it away.

"Well, you were all just standing there," Paul continued. "Andy, the call was real. But you have to admit, it wasn't. Know what I'm saying? The girl's alive. And she doesn't believe it either, right?"

"Freaks out every time I talk to her."

Paul looked slyly at Andy. "She really good-looking?"

In spite of his mood Andy grinned. "Yeah," he admitted.

They both laughed.

"Forget her," Paul said, stretching out his

legs and lifting his face to the sun. "She's too old for you. How you doing with Sally?"

"Okay," Andy replied, though he hadn't thought much about her lately. "I'm just worried . . ."

"Andy, the guy was nuts. Besides, there's nothing you can do to make people believe you."

"That's what the cop said: 'Give me something to believe.' If she got killed, they'd believe."

"Man, if you talk like that they'll really bust your ass."

"I'd like to find him . . ."

"You don't know anything about him. I mean, you said his call was a coincidence."

"Maybe it wasn't."

"Come on! Why should he call you? Might be anyone. From anywhere. California! Or New York. Piles of freaks out there. You don't know *anything*."

"He was local," Andy insisted.

The next-period bell rang.

"Okay," said Paul, coming to his feet. "Say you found the sucker. Then what? I mean, what would you do, really?"

Andy groped for an answer. "I don't know," he admitted.

"Want my advice?"

"What?"

"Forget it."

"Why does everyone say that?"

"Because no one else is as dumb as you."

At the apartment Andy's father greeted him with, "Anything else happen in school?"

"No," said Andy. "You speak to the lawyer?"

"He's out of town. Have an appointment for Tuesday."

Andy started for his room, saying, "Boy, I'd really like to find out who Zeke is . . ."

"Andy!"

"What?"

"Please. I meant it. No more. Is that understood?"

Andy murmured a sulky "yes."

"And I made some changes in my plans for tonight."

"I told you . . ."

"Sorry. I don't feel comfortable leaving you. I invited Peggy here."

"You're kidding."

"Got some lobsters in the fridge. That okay

with you? And I thought we could take in a movie."

Andy knew it wasn't okay but also knew that if he said anything his father would only be more upset with him. This date was important. "Sure. Fine," he said.

"And do me a favor," his father added. "No talk about this business, you hear?"

"Can I *think* about it?"

"Andy . . ."

"I'm not that dumb," said Andy. He retreated into his room, convinced his father was ashamed of him.

/ Peggy Anderson came into the apartment as if she'd been there all her life, chatting nonstop in a slight Texas drawl. Rather small, she was full of energy and motion. To Andy's watchful eye she dressed in an arty fashion.

Dr. Zadinski was awkward as he tried to please her and Andy at the same time. But he was full of smiles and laughter in ways Andy hadn't seen for a long while.

During dinner Peggy and his father tried to include Andy in the conversation. But somehow his father's admonition not to talk about what was uppermost in his thoughts—the need to get people to understand the Zeke thing was real—made him feel reserved, not part of the dinner at all. Instead, he kept his distance, taking pleasure in the fact that they had no idea what was on his mind.

From time to time he glanced at his father, wondering if he had forgotten the whole business.

In the middle of dessert the phone rang. Dr. Zadinski answered it. "It's for you," he told Andy, whispering, "a girl."

Andy took the call in his father's room. "Hello?"

"It's me, Sally."

"Oh, hi," said Andy, glad to hear from her.

"We were going over to the Mall. Thought you'd like to come."

"Can't."

"How come?"

"My father . . . he's going out with this woman he met. A date. Only she's here. He wants me home."

"Your father, dating?" Sally giggled.

"Yeah."

"What's she like?"

"I don't know. I just met her."

Sally lowered her voice. "He going to marry her?"

"He just met her."

"If my mother or father were, you know, dating, I don't know if I could handle it. Can't even see it."

They both laughed.

"I heard about the cop," she said.

"It's nothing."

"That call thing?"

"Sort of . . ."

"What's happened now?"

Andy remembered his father's cautions. "I don't want to talk about it," he said. There was an awkward pause.

"Well, just thought I'd ask about the Mall."

"Thanks."

"Speak to you later."

They hung up. For a moment Andy thought of asking his father about going to the Mall. It would be good to talk it out with Sally.

But his father called: "Andy! Movie in twenty minutes. We gotta go!"

Andy, for his father's sake, went with them.

/Next morning, when Andy woke, he tried to plan out the day, wanting to do something to take his mind off the call business. He decided to put his bike into shape.

He was still working on it when his father came outside.

"It's too nice to hang around," his father said. "How about a ride out by the lake? I can use the exercise."

There were only three cars in the Lake Hammondy parking lot when they got there.

"It's going to rain," Andy predicted, looking up at the clouds which were building to the west.

"We're not going far."

There was a big path circling the lake, a smooth, eight-mile tar surface of loops and straightaways. Andy and Paul liked to race it.

"Want to race?" his father asked as they started off side by side.

Andy didn't give an answer. Instead, he crouched over, gripped the drop handles, and began to pedal hard.

"Hey," his father called. "No fair!"

Pressing harder, Andy slipped into low gear for maximum power.

He took the first curve at a hard angle, the straightaways even faster. His heart pumped, his muscles strained.

When he took a quick look over his shoulder, his father was no longer in sight.

Anticipating the hill ahead, Andy shifted gears and kept his cadence. He looked back again at the summit to see his father pumping along below.

Andy accelerated downhill, shifting back into low gear, daring himself not to squeeze the brakes. He felt as if he were flying.

To his left, a gap in the trees allowed him to see the lake. There was hardly a ripple, and out toward the middle, a canoe with a couple bobbed. In front of him, Andy could see the first of the swimming areas where the county had created a beach by dumping tons of sand. He brought the bike to an easy stop alongside the water fountain there, leaned over to take a drink, then stopped and looked toward the beach.

A barefooted woman was walking at the water's edge. To Andy's astonishment he saw that it was Nina.

She was wearing a cape that billowed white against the dark lake waters, moving as though in a dance, lifting her bare feet slowly, arching them, her arms out from her sides, fingers spread wide, head tilted back toward the sky, her eyes tightly closed. Andy noticed she was wearing a headset with the cassette player strapped to her waist.

He stood perfectly still, staring at her, thinking how beautiful she was, before he realized that anybody could have been in his place, watching as he was—even Zeke.

The thought jolted him.

Andy wanted to warn Nina, tell her not to come to such an isolated place alone. But afraid of her reaction, he stayed still.

Perhaps his father could tell her.

But Andy didn't want to remind his father about the Zeke thing. They'd had a good evening, and a good morning, because he had kept quiet.

Hurriedly, Andy pushed on, pedaling until he went around a bend, a point from which he could no longer see Nina, nor she him if she looked. There, pretending to adjust his gears, he waited.

/His father was gasping as he rode up. "You'll have . . . to go . . . slower. No way . . . I can keep up . . . I'm really . . . out of shape."

At the far side they left their bikes and walked

to the lake's edge. A frog plopped into the water. Mid-lake, the canoe was heading for shore, paddles flashing in a steady beat. It had grown darker.

"We should do this more often," Andy's father said.

Andy couldn't get the image of Nina out of his mind.

"I know it's a mob scene in August," his father said. "But now . . ." He gestured toward the canoe. "Except for those people, it's just us."

Andy looked across the water toward the beach area. He couldn't see Nina.

"Who's cooking tonight?" Dr. Zadinski asked.

"Me."

"I'll be hungry. You know something?"

"What?"

"I like doing this kind of thing with you."

"Really," said Andy.

As they reached the car, rain began to fall. Quickly, they lashed their bikes to the car rack. When they pulled out only one car remained in the lot. "April showers," said Dr. Zadinski. "Someone's going to get wet."

Andy looked at the remaining car closely. It was a red Ford. An Escort. In his head, Andy heard the voice of Zeke. He shivered.

/The phone was ringing when they came into the apartment. Andy hurried to get it.

"Is Robert there?"

"Just a second." Andy held the phone out to his father. "Peggy," he announced.

Dr. Zadinski's face brightened into a smile. "Hi," he said to her. "No, sure. Wait a moment. Here, Andy. Hang this up when I get on." He went into his own room.

Andy lifted the phone to his ear. His father picked up the extension.

"Okay, Andy, I'm on."

Andy hesitated. He wanted to blurt out what he had seen, what he feared might happen.

"Andy?" his father prompted.

Andy hung up and went into the living room and lay down on the couch. The image of Nina by the lake held him.

/That night his father allowed him to go to the Mall with Paul. A reward, Andy figured. Paul's mother drove them, making sure they knew when and where she'd pick them up.

The boys went to the regular meeting place, the central fountain. Other kids were already there, and during the evening as many as fifty showed up.

Andy kept his eyes open for Sally, hoping she'd come so he could talk to her about seeing Nina. He considered telling Paul, but held back, wary of Paul treating the whole thing as a joke.

Once, when he went to get a slice of pizza, he passed a group of kids from his school. "Hey, Zadinski," one of them called, "get any more wacko calls?"

Although uncomfortable, Andy grinned and waved.

Sally never came.

/When he got back home he found a note on the kitchen table.

I'm at Peggy's—387-3842

Dad

Andy studied the note and, uneasy, glanced at the phone. *I just killed someone,* Zeke said in his head, as if the voice were trapped inside.

Andy thought of Nina alone by the lake. If she kept doing things like that something awful would happen. And it would be his fault.

He went into his room and put music on,

thinking about the various conversations he
had had with other people, until something
his father had mentioned momentarily grew
large, only to fade. Sensing its importance, he
tried to hang on to it. His father . . . their
number . . . the note . . . the call.

Suddenly he made the connection: Didn't his
father say that he'd written their new number
and left it on the Math Department secretary's
desk that Friday?

He had . . .

Andy tried to grasp what that could mean.
Gradually the question became clear. *What had
the math secretary done with that note?*

/Andy was eating breakfast
reading the Sunday sports pages, when his father
came into the kitchen.

" 'Morning," his father said, cheerful and full
of energy.

" 'Morning," Andy returned.

His father set about making his own breakfast. "How are things at the Mall?" he asked.

"Fine," said Andy, putting his paper aside.
"Can I ask you something?"

"Sure." He was busy at the stove.

"That Friday night, when you gave your departmental secretary our new phone number, what did she do with it?"

Dr. Zadinski said nothing.

"Dad? You hear me?"

When his father turned around Andy realized he was angry. "What's the matter?" Andy asked.

"In the first place," said Dr. Zadinski, "I didn't say I gave it to her. I told you, distinctly, that I left it on her desk. She was gone. In the second, much more important place, we are waiting to see if someone is bringing a . . . a morals charge against you. You may have forgotten. I haven't. Can't you get it into your head that *that* is something to worry about, not that damned call. We spend a perfectly nice day—yesterday. No idiotic talk. No problems. I thought we were done with it. Then . . . bang! Here we go again. You promised you'd lay off."

"I haven't done anything," said Andy. "It's just—"

"How many times do I have to say it," his father said, "it's all in *your* head!"

Andy, stung, said, "You'd believe me fast enough if I showed you who Zeke was!"

"That's absurd."

"Dad, someone is out there talking about killing a person. I might know how to find the guy, keep it from happening."

"In the first place, nothing is going to happen. In the second, if there really is such a person, he's crazy. A psychopath. Dangerous."

"Right! So people should do nothing. Is that what you're saying? If the guy had some disease, busted a leg, or was starving, you'd want me to help, right? Nina Klemmer is in danger!"

Dr. Zadinski started to say something, but instead turned back to the stove.

"Well?" challenged Andy.

His father said, "We need to clean up around here. And make out a cooking schedule for the week. That okay with you, Sherlock?"

"You don't know what I'm onto, do you?"

"Andy, you've got good motives. But what started out as something . . . merely unpleasant, has gotten out of hand. How many times do I have to tell you: Leave it be!"

/ Andy lay on his bed, the music blaring, thinking about the Mathematics Department office. You stepped into it from a big hallway. The secretary had her desk outside the chairperson's office. At the other end of her desk was the entrance to a large meeting room where all the departmental gatherings were held. It had to be there—that Friday— where the meeting his father went to took place.

According to his father, he left the meeting first, and fast, rushing to get to the Fillmores' for dinner. It was then that he left the phone number on the secretary's desk. Except, *she had gone*. His father just said that. So the number was lying there.

But then, afterward, all the *other* people from the meeting would have passed by. *They would have gone by the desk.* Someone could have seen that piece of paper with the number on it and picked it up.

And that night someone called.

/ By two o'clock in the afternoon the house jobs had been completed. When his father went out to do some shopping Andy took the college phone book into his own room and closed his door.

Each section of the book was made up of different colored papers, one for each school or department. Administration, green. The

President's office, purple. The Math Department, orange.

Listed for the Math Department were twenty-seven faculty names, last names first, their office numbers and phones. Also listed were faculty titles: Instructor, Assistant, Associate, or Professor. For each: Dr., Ms., Mrs., or Mr.

Zeke's was a male voice, so Andy discounted the four women in the department.

He studied the remaining twenty-three names. Many were familiar. A few men were friends of his father's. He tried to recollect their faces, their voices, anything about them. It was very little.

Andy acknowledged that Zeke didn't have to be one of these people, or be from the department at all—that it was only a guess.

Still . . . Nina Klemmer came from the college. That was the one fact he had.

Andy smiled. "Sherlock," his father had called him, sarcastically. Okay, Andy thought, why not?

Part Three

Monday morning Andy got a message reminding him that during eighth period, his normal study hall, Mrs. Baskin was expecting him. His first thought was that Nina had filed charges after all. Anticipating the worst, he went to her office.

"Andy," she began, her voice soft, almost a whisper. "I spoke to Officer Dorfman. I don't know if he'll be getting in touch with you or your father, but as of this morning, that young woman had not filed formal charges. He doesn't think she will."

Andy sat back and sighed.

"But this isn't over yet," Mrs. Baskin was quick to say. "She can still bring charges, and from what I've been told, she will, if . . ." She left the *if* to dangle.

"If what?"

"If you bother her in any way at all again."

"I never was bothering her."

Mrs. Baskin frowned. "Andy, I'm going to be very direct with you. By your own admission you called her, a perfect stranger, twice, harassed her in the college library, persisted in harassing her at the college student building, even used force . . ."

"But . . ."

"Andy, I want you to listen to me."

"But what about that guy?"

Mrs. Baskin shook her head. "Andy, no more."

Andy slumped down and stared at the ceiling.

"Now," Mrs. Baskin continued, "I've done some checking. Your grades seem fine. You appear to have a good number of friends. I don't see any problems in school. How are things at home?"

"Fine."

Mrs. Baskin considered that for a moment. "Are you sure?" she probed.

"Yes."

Again she lapsed into thought. Then she said, "I'd still like you to come by on Mondays during study hall period for a brief chat these next few weeks."

Andy continued to stare at the ceiling.

"Andy," she said, "it would be much better if you talked about things. To bottle them up only hurts you."

"What's the point," he told her. "No one believes me."

"I do."

"About *everything?*"

"Andy, you're being trusted. No one is punishing you. You're under no restraints. But let me remind you—as a friend, Andy—if *anything* else happens you'll likely find yourself in serious trouble."

"What if I could prove the thing about Zeke?" said Andy.

"Don't," returned Mrs. Baskin.

/ As soon as Andy got home he brought the phone into his room. On one side of it he placed his notebook in which he had written his questions—a fake survey for the town newspaper. On the other side he put the list of people he was going to call.

With a deep breath he edged forward in his chair and called the first number. As it rang, he nervously wiped his free hand on his shirt to get rid of the sweat.

"Hello?" It was a woman's voice.

"Can I speak to Dr. Carlos Boros?"

"Who's calling, please?"

"Peter Smith," said Andy. "I'm taking a survey."

"Just a moment, please. He's out back." The phone clattered down and Andy waited, growing increasingly tense.

"Hello?" It was a new voice. A man's.

"Is this Dr. Carlos Boros?"

"Yes, it is?"

"This is Peter Smith, and I'm doing a survey for the Madison *Times*. Do you take it?"

"Yes, I do."

"I'd . . . I'd like to ask you what you think of it?"

"Well," said Dr. Boros, "it's all right, I suppose . . ."

Andy, deciding it was not Zeke he was hearing, abruptly hung up. Only then did he realize he'd been holding his breath.

/ "Hello?" A woman's voice.

"Can I speak to Mr. Jack Irwin?"

"Sorry. He's not in. Can I take a message?"

"That's all right," said Andy. "I'll call back."

/ It was close to four-thirty when he made his fifteenth call.

"Hello?"

"Can I speak to Dr. Philip Lucas?"

"Speaking."

Andy felt as if someone had slammed him in the stomach. It was Zeke's voice he was hearing.

"This . . . this is Peter Smith," he managed to say, his heart hammering.

"Who did you say?"

"Peter . . . Smith."

"Yes, Mr. Smith. What can I do for you?"

"I'm . . . I'm doing a survey for the Madison *Times*. Do you take it?" Andy's voice kept breaking.

"Yes."

"Can I ask you what you think of it?"

For a moment Dr. Lucas said nothing. "Sir?" said Andy, thinking he might have lost him.

"Who is this?" asked Lucas.

"Peter Smith," said Andy. Then he remembered with horror that it was the name he'd given when Zeke called.

"*Whom* do you represent?"

"The . . . newspaper," Andy faltered. "I'm taking a survey, and—"

"I'm not interested in such things," said Lucas and hung up.

Stunned, Andy held the phone until it began to beep. Then he put it down and buried his head in his arms, attempting to recapture the voice he had just heard. Zeke's voice. Dr. Philip Lucas's voice. They were the same.

Certain his father had mentioned Lucas, Andy struggled to recall something about the man. He came up with nothing. He wondered if he had ever seen him. No picture came to mind.

And what if I'm wrong? he asked himself.

Andy reached for the phone and began to punch in Lucas's number, only to drop the receiver quickly. He was trembling.

He forced himself to check the next name on the list. Hurriedly, almost in a panic, he called, conscious of his desire that he wanted someone else, anyone, to sound like Zeke. But by the time he had made all the calls, only one fit: Dr. Philip Lucas.

/ Andy was in the kitchen finishing a salad when Dr. Zadinski came home. "How're you doing?" his father called from the door.

"Fine," said Andy, without turning around. He had been dreading the moment he had to confront him with what he had learned. Just the thought of it made him feel ill.

"Sorry I'm late," his father said. "How was your day?"

"Nothing special," Andy replied.

"Be right there. Just want to wash up."

"Take your time."

After a moment Dr. Zadinski called, "I heard from Mrs. Baskin this afternoon. . . ." He came into the kitchen and began to set the table. "She told me that the student hasn't pressed charges so far. And the police—according to her—aren't pushing her to do so either."

Andy nodded.

"So I called the lawyer's office to cancel my appointment. That should make you feel good."

Andy, more and more upset, began to serve

the dinner. His father looked at him, but said nothing.

The food served, Andy sat opposite his father.

"Andy," Dr. Zadinski said finally, "look at me."

Andy looked up, tears running down his face. "What's the matter?"

"Zeke is real," Andy said, unable to keep it back. The words came out half choked.

His father stared at him, then shook his head sadly. "What can I do to get you off this?"

Andy gulped for breath. "All I'm . . . saying . . . is that . . . someone . . . should tell her . . . she's going to get . . . killed."

"Andy," his father said, "give me one iota of objective proof. *One.*"

Andy, afraid to tell his father what he had found out, pushed himself away from the table and fled into his room.

He lay on his bed staring at nothing. Through the walls he listened to his father's muffled, agitated voice on the phone to Peggy. After a moment Andy crawled to the foot of his bed and eased the door open a crack.

". . . exactly," he heard his father say. "The kid is caught up in a fantasy."

Andy shut the door and pressed his face into

his pillow. "I wish," he cried to himself, "I wish I didn't know!"

/In class the next day Andy could hardly pay attention. Instead, he sat in the far back doodling in his notebook: *Zeke . . . Nina . . . Lucas.* The letters were elongated, twisted, endlessly linked to one another. Sometimes he inserted his own name.

Vague notions of trying to warn Nina again kept edging into his mind. As did thoughts about asking his father about Lucas.

Then Andy realized that before he said or did anything else he had to be one hundred percent certain he was right about Lucas. With that in mind he headed for Brazell Hall at the college as soon as school let out.

A note tacked to Dr. Zadinski's door explained he was at a meeting. Relieved, Andy slipped past, along the hall where, next to the departmental office, there was a wall chart on which all of the professors' office numbers were listed. Dr. Lucas had Room B-316.

The door to Lucas's office was locked. Andy made a fast check of the schedule posted on it and discovered Lucas was teaching Math 520 in Room M-56. The first student he met told him where he could find the place.

/ Minkoff Hall was a classroom building, its rooms arranged in sequence. The one Andy wanted was easy to locate. Through a door window he could see that a class was in session, and fortunately, the entrance was at the back of the room.

Wishing his heart would calm down, Andy put his hand on the door handle, rehearsing once more the story he'd concocted in case of a challenge.

As he entered the class, everyone in the room, including Lucas, who was writing on the blackboard, turned. "Yes?" Lucas said, peering over a pair of glasses that had slipped to the end of his nose. He tapped them back up.

Andy said, "A friend of mine asked me, uh, to take notes for him." His voice quavered. "He's sick."

Lucas considered Andy for a moment, then swung back to the board. As he continued to write and talk, the students shifted their attention back to him. Andy took the nearest seat.

When Lucas finished writing and faced the class, Andy got his first really good look at him.

Lucas was in his fifties, older than Andy's father. He was slimmer, too. His suit was brown, perfectly fitted. Andy decided his shirt was tinted gray. His tie was held in place with an elegant tie clasp, and when he lifted his arms, fancy cufflinks flashed.

Dr. Lucas's face was as composed as his clothing, smooth-shaven, pink, with few lines—it reminded Andy of a baby's face. His thick, dark hair, combed back with a slight wave, was gray at the temples. When he talked to the class he stood very still. His steady eyes, behind slightly tinted glasses, appeared completely earnest, focusing now on this student, now that. His voice was soft, low, persistent.

Lucas didn't look at all as Andy had imagined him. Just the opposite. In front of the room stood a calm, dignified man.

What impressed Andy most was his command of the class. No one spoke out of turn. All Andy could hear—save for Lucas's voice—Zeke's voice—was the occasional creak of a shifting chair, the scratch of pencil on paper.

/No bell sounded to end the class. Everyone seemed to know exactly when the time was up.

Lucas made his final remarks, something about the date of a future exam, and homework to be done and collected. Then, hands clasped, he watched over the students as they made for the door.

Andy scrambled up. But when he turned to take one last look he discovered Lucas was gazing right at him.

"Young man," said Lucas. "Would you please stay."

Taken by surprise, Andy stopped where he was, watching the other students leave. He felt like calling out for help. But in moments they were gone.

"Now then," said Lucas, calmly but firmly, "you said you came to take notes for a sick friend. What friend? You took no notes."

"I think I made a mistake," Andy stammered out. "See, my friend was sick and he asked me to sit in on his class. Only I don't think it's this one. I didn't mean to bother you."

Lucas kept his eyes on Andy. "Who was the instructor?" he asked.

Andy felt himself getting red.

"*Do* you know the name?" insisted Lucas.

"Dr. Zadinski," Andy got out.

"Ah," said Lucas. "Then you do indeed have

the wrong class." He turned to the table where his papers were and began to gather them up.

Andy wasn't sure what to do.

Lucas looked at him over his shoulder. "You may go," he said.

/ "What's the matter?" said Dr. Zadinski when he realized Andy wasn't eating his dinner.

"Dad," Andy began, looking down. "What . . . what if I . . . I told you . . . I know . . . who Zeke is?"

When his father said nothing, Andy peeked up. Dr. Zadinski's face was flushed with anger.

"How many times have you promised me that you'd drop this?" he said, speaking with great deliberation.

"I know who he is," Andy whispered.

Dr. Zadinski thrust himself away from the table, got up, and walked into the living room, his hands deep in his pockets. Andy watched anxiously.

"I don't want to hear," his father said.

Andy felt sick.

"I mean," his father continued, "I don't know what you've done now. Frankly, I'm afraid to ask. All I *do* know is that again and again you've promised . . ." He stopped what he was about to say, shook his head, and dropped onto the living room couch. Andy watched from the table.

"Please come here," his father said.

Feeling like a little boy about to be punished, Andy reluctantly did as he was told. His father gestured him to a chair. "Sit down," he said.

Andy sat. Dr. Zadinski stared at him. Then he said, "Did you or did you not promise to lay off?"

"Yes, but . . ."

"Yes or no?"

"Sort of . . ."

His father leaned forward out of the couch. "How am I . . . how are *we* going to trust each other if you keep making promises then keep breaking them?"

"I had to find out, Dad. I had to."

"When you've been warned, told, even threatened?"

"The other day," said Andy, "when we were biking, she was there, *alone*. She could have been killed."

Dr. Zadinski's eyes got very big. "Who are you talking about?"

"Nina."

His father said nothing. He just looked at Andy.

"Don't you care?" Andy asked.

Dr. Zadinski folded his arms over his chest and sat back. "No," he said, shaking his head. "I'm not the slightest bit interested."

"Not interested . . ." Andy echoed.

"Andy, let's get this straight. I believe someone called you that Friday. I believe there's a young woman named Nina Klemmer who is a student at my college. *But it was a crank call.* Okay, an obscene call. But it's not to be taken seriously. You've become obsessed. Absolutely obsessed. It has got to stop! It's impossible to believe *anything* you say anymore. This girl . . . at the lake." He shook his head. "Andy, no one was there. We even talked about how empty the place was. You are living in some kind of fantasy world without one shred of evidence to support your insane notions!"

"I do have evidence!"

"What? Come on. Give it to me!"

"Dr. Lucas," Andy blurted out.

"I beg your pardon."

"Dr. Philip Lucas," repeated Andy with a sense of great release.

Dr. Zadinski looked blank. "What does Phil Lucas have to do with this conversation?"

"*That's* Zeke," said Andy. "The one who called!"

Andy's father opened his mouth in surprise.

"He took our number from the secretary's desk when you left it there after that meeting. I've worked it all out. Don't you see? It's true. I even spoke to him on the phone. Dad, he's got Zeke's voice. *Exactly. You* said it was a phony name. Well, it was. I went to one of his classes—today!—and listened. He's the same person. See, I do have proof." Andy sat back, relieved to have it out.

Dr. Zadinski considered for a while. Then he said, "Andy, let me tell you something about Phil Lucas. In the first place, he's a friend of mine. I have known him for as long as I've been at Madison. He helped hire me. Get me tenure. He's been around for years—much, much longer than I. A *highly* respected colleague. Not just in my department, but all over the place. He's written I don't know how many textbooks. He's a particular friend of the college president. Gets merit pay each year. Important. As things go there, powerful . . . He was at that party we went to a couple of Saturdays ago."

"He was?" said Andy, surprised.

"Yes, because people like him. Admire him. Do you know why? He comes from a background of rural poverty. Who knows what he had to go through to get where he is now. Whatever it took, he did it. He's smart. Soft-spoken. He's got a sense of humor. A nice, decent sort of person. Oh, he's a fancy dresser, with his suits and those fancy cufflinks of his. And well off. Gets a new car every couple of years. Nor is he married. Let's hope that's no mark against him. . . . That you would pick him," said Dr. Zadinski, his voice rising in scorn, "pick him from all the people you might fancifully select is—I think—frankly—obscene. I mean, *really* obscene. Yet you . . . what did you say? You called him? You went to one of his classes? Spied on him? When did you do this?"

Andy leaned forward and covered his eyes with his hands. He could feel tears rising.

"I asked you a question," his father said.

"This afternoon," said Andy, his voice small.

"Did you tell him who you were?"

Andy shook his head.

"Does he have any idea you're my son?"

Andy shook his head once more.

"I'll tell you something: I have no faith in

your judgment. None. Did you give him any inkling of your . . . extraordinary . . . conclusion?"

Totally miserable, Andy managed to get out a "no."

"Let's be thankful for small mercies," his father said, sitting back, hands on his knees, looking at Andy as if he were a stranger. Leaning from the couch he said, "May I ask you . . . what you intend to do with this . . . this . . . notion?"

"I don't know yet."

"Yet!" his father lashed out.

"I don't!" Andy yelled back.

"Andy," said his father, a note of pleading creeping into his voice. "Do you have *any* idea of the possible consequences of what you're doing? If you . . . go public with this . . . insane, cockamamie piece of . . . fantasy?"

"I don't care," cried Andy, feeling as though he was being taunted.

"Exactly," returned his father. "And do you have any idea what position you might be putting me—or my job—in?"

Andy shook his head.

After a while his father said, "Andy, I think . . . and I say this with a whole lot of love . . . because you are my son . . . and I do love you. I really, truly do. But, my God, you're a very mixed-up young man. And I don't know how to help you."

"You still don't believe me, do you?"

His father laughed a big, full, rolling laugh. "Is that a serious question?" he asked.

"It's all true!" Andy screamed at him.

"It-is-not-true!" Dr. Zadinski returned, just as fiercely, making Andy jump. "It's a load of crazy crap. Nina Klemmer at the lake . . . I was *there*, Andy, right by your side. If she was there, why didn't you point her out to me? I'm not blind."

"I was scared to," cried Andy.

"Bull! When have you ever been scared of me before? After all we've been through. Oh, come on! . . . As for Phil Lucas being this . . . Zeke! It is absolutely, one hundred percent— one hundred and ten percent—insane! You are nuts!"

Andy bent over his knees and began to sob.

His father remained sitting, helpless. He started to reach forward only to drop back into the couch, tears in his own eyes. Then he got up, circled around Andy, and put his hands on his son's shoulders, squeezing and kneading them lovingly. "Look here, kid," he said, his voice husky. "I don't know what you and I are going to do about all this. You need help. Oh, my God, do you need help. More than Mrs. Baskin can give you. Maybe *I* need help. I'm beginning to think so. Maybe we need it together." He struggled to keep himself calm.

"For the moment I think you had better go into your room and let me alone. I'm afraid of saying the wrong thing. Something I'll be sorry for. I already have. The same for you. Go on. Do it," he said softly, giving Andy a small push. "Scoot."

Andy wiped his face clear of tears and managed to get up. From somewhere he found one more bit of strength to try to explain. "Dad," he began, "the reason I didn't tell you about Nina at the lake . . ."

Dr. Zadinski held up his hand, as if protecting himself from being hit. "Andy . . . no more. I have to think this through. Just go to your room and *please*, think about what you're saying, and doing . . ."

Andy went. If his father said what people believed, then he, Andy, was the only person who knew Lucas for what he was, a potential killer. The thought filled him with a sense of horror. At his desk, he buried his face in his arms, fighting back the tears.

/In the morning, neither Andy nor his father spoke. Instead, each went through his regular routines as if the other weren't there. Only when Andy was about to leave for school did his father call out.

"Andy!"

Andy paused.

"Make absolutely certain," his father said, his voice hard and unnatural to Andy's ears, "that *nothing* happens today. Is that clear?"

"Okay," Andy said automatically.

"I'll be asking you at dinner. By then, I'll be able to tell you what my plans are."

"What plans?"

"What I intend to do about all this."

Andy waited for him to say more, but his father only turned away.

/School was actually a relief. Andy got involved in classes, found himself interested, did well. He even got a good grade on a biology quiz, which clinched a decent midterm grade.

Paul met him for lunch. "Tryouts tomorrow," he reminded Andy. "We should practice this afternoon."

"Got work to do," Andy told him.

"Are you serious?"

"Just keep off my case, will you," Andy snapped, and started off.

"What's the matter now?" Paul called after him.

Andy, wishing he hadn't spoken so hastily, kept walking.

After school he biked to the college, wanting to hide in his library corner and do work. Then, if he were asked what he'd done, he'd be able to say what his father liked to hear. It might help.

He locked up his bike, then hurried to his regular spot, the soft chair next to the window overlooking the parking lot. Quickly, he settled in but noticed a red car come into the lot. It took a while for the driver to find a place, and Andy watched it with amusement. But when the driver stepped out, it was Nina Klemmer.

As always, she was dressed boldly, a golden yellow dress, long and free-flowing. She wore a straw hat, too, from which bright ribbons dangled. In her arms she carried a bundle of books.

As she came toward the library Andy watched, fascinated. Whether or not she entered the building, he couldn't tell. He assumed she did.

At the same moment Andy remembered two

things: his promise to his father not to do anything, and his own certainty that he knew who
Zeke was. If he could get Nina on his side . . .

He snatched up his things and headed for
the stairwell, rehearsing what he might say. But
no sooner did he start down the steps, than
Nina appeared on the bottom landing.

Andy froze.

Nina, halfway up, sensed someone above and
stopped. When she saw Andy, a fleeting look
of fear came to her face.

"I . . . found out who he is . . ." Andy said.

Nina stared at him.

"Don't you want to hear?" Andy said, almost
pleading.

Nina's look of fear faded. "Why are you doing
this?" she said.

"Doing what?"

"This stalking me. Pestering me. I mean, I
know you. The last time this happened I called
the police."

"I'm . . . trying to help," Andy stammered.

"Help with what?"

"You."

"That's the oldest line in the book."

"It's not a line. If you'd just let me tell you
who—"

"You know," she said, cutting him off, "when

you started this I got upset. I was wrong. I mean, why don't you just bug off . . . jerk!" She stepped against the stairwell wall, one hand clutching her books, the other hand holding back her skirt to let Andy pass, as if he were something dirty.

Andy went down the steps silently. At the landing he stopped and turned.

"I'm trying to save you!" he cried out.

With a flamboyant turn that set her skirt whirling, she hurried up the steps.

Andy watched her go, feeling a helpless shame.

At home the silence of the morning continued. Dinner was glum and tense, though from time to time Dr. Zadinski made a feeble effort to talk. Each time it failed.

When dinner was over Andy excused himself from the table and started to clean up. But his father said, "Andy, sit down. We need to talk." There was a nervous rasp to his voice.

With a sense of defeat Andy slumped into a chair, prepared for the worst.

"I've thought about this whole . . . business," his father began. "Considered it every which way. I've talked to people, too."

"Who, Peggy?"

"Just listen," his father said, refusing to be provoked. He picked up a napkin, folded it a few times, pressed it flat with his fingers. "I think it would be . . . good . . . if both of us could get away for a while. From Madison. You know, a trip. A vacation. Change of scene. But I can't. Not until the term ends. That's two months."

"I've got school, too," Andy reminded him.

His father seemed to consider the point but then he said, "Maybe it would be better if you went away now."

"Are you serious?"

"I've spoken to your school . . . Mrs. Baskin. They're being understanding and cooperative. You're doing well, academically. A week or two won't make much of a difference. Not in the long run. Anyway, you'll bring along school assignments, readings, things to keep up. I called your Aunt Mary. I know you've always enjoyed visiting down there. She'd love to have you. Take a week. Or two. More if you'd like. As long as you need."

The room became very still.

"You mean it, don't you?" said Andy.

"Yes."

"I've got baseball tryouts tomorrow."

"You'll have to forget about it until you get back."

Andy wanted to pick up the chair he was sitting on and smash it. "Why?" he managed.

"To get you out of a rut. To get you away from . . . all of this, whatever *this* is. I don't pretend to know. This business about the call, the girl, has become some kind of addiction. It's got to be broken off—cold turkey—before you do real harm. You don't seem to be able to stop it yourself. Am I wrong about that?"

Andy looked away, thinking about his afternoon meeting with Nina.

"I can't be with you every moment," Dr. Zadinski continued. "Anyway, you'll have fun on Mary's farm. You know how much she dotes on you. And . . . maybe . . . you need to get away from me, too. It has been a rough year. Your mom's death. Selling the house. Moving. I don't know what else. At least, that's what I'm thinking. Last week when all this began, you said you'd like to be far away."

"You're punishing me for finding out the truth," said Andy.

His father shook his head. "I am not punishing you. And you haven't found the truth. I am helping you."

"I don't want to go," Andy said.

His father took a deep breath. "Andy, I'm not asking. I am telling you."

Andy sprang up from his chair, trying to find a way out. "When?" he asked.

"When I spoke to Mary and told her about . . . what's happening . . . I did have to tell her," Dr. Zadinski said apologetically, "she said she'd love to have you right away. But not this weekend. Showing cattle or something. I'll make plane reservations for Tuesday." He looked bleakly at Andy. "I'm going to miss you," he said, the coolness in his voice finally breaking.

Andy stormed into his room, slamming the door behind him. All he could think about was that he had to put up or shut up, fast. But there was so little time. . . .

On Thursday, between his classes, Paul confronted him. "We've got tryouts today."

"Not me."

"Andy, what is going *on*?"

"I'm being sent away."

"Are you serious?"

"Yeah."

"Why?"

"I don't want to talk about it," Andy said, and walked off.

After school he returned to an empty apartment. At first he didn't enter. Instead, he stood in the doorway and gazed at the sunlight pouring through the windows. The rooms seemed filled with bits of dust endlessly churning upon themselves, as his feelings churned.

Dumping his books to the floor, he dropped on the couch, then rolled over on his stomach, cheek to pillow, one arm dangling, letting his fingers brush the hardwood floor. All he could think of was his failure to get people to see how dangerous Lucas was.

"Nuts," his father called him.

"Jerk," said Nina.

"Dumb," said Paul.

The only person he hadn't tried to get help from was Lucas himself.

With a feeling of helplessness, Andy paced the apartment. He looked for food but found nothing to satisfy an appetite he didn't have. He searched closets without knowing what he sought. He thought of rearranging his room only to give it up. . . .

Was it . . . in any way possible . . . *could he,*

get Lucas to help? Andy sat down and tried to think it through. What . . . what if he could . . . force . . . Lucas into the open . . . by letting him know . . . someone . . . had discovered the truth. A kind of . . . blackmail.

Not really blackmail, Andy quickly told himself. No money was involved. Nothing like that. No, Lucas would pay by . . . being Zeke . . . in public.

Andy tried to find a flaw. A catch. He couldn't. On the contrary, the more he considered the idea, the greater its possibilities grew, the more certain he became that he'd stumbled on the solution to his problem.

After all, he told himself, he knew who Zeke was, but Lucas knew nothing of him. From perfect safety—by phone—he could pressure Lucas. Lucas would act while he, Andy, kept his distance. A *safe* distance, and he wouldn't be getting involved. Just what he promised his father. In fact, all he needed to do was decide with whom he wanted Lucas to be Zeke.

For the first time since he had his idea, Andy hesitated. The obvious person was Nina. If she complained when Andy did nothing, she'd really scream when Lucas talked to her. People would have to believe her.

But wasn't that risky? he asked himself.

Once more he felt the pressure of time. It was the only way. The fastest way. The way that would, in the end, protect Nina best.

Andy went into his father's room, opened the college phone book, and looked up Lucas's number and wrote it down. Then he brought the phone into his own room and carefully shut the door and locked it.

But after putting the phone on his desk, he felt a loss of nerve. Do it, he kept telling himself. Do it! It's the only way!

Slowly, heart hammering, conscious of his fear but at the same time telling himself he would be a coward not to act, that there was no time to do anything else, that he had to protect people from Lucas, that he wouldn't be involved, that this was his last chance . . . he pressed out the correct numbers with a trembling hand and held the phone to his ear.

"Hello."

Andy recognized Lucas instantly. "That you . . . Zeke?" he said.

Lucas gave a sharp intake of breath. To Andy it was the unmistakable sound of being discovered.

Louder, bolder, he said, "It *is* you, Zeke, isn't it?"

Lucas hung up.

Andy stayed by his phone, his excitement growing. A great weight seemed to roll off him. Sending his chair crashing, he leaped into the air as if spearing a line drive. At last he had done something right. As far as he was concerned—there was not the slightest doubt —Lucas's reaction was proof that he was vulnerable. He got me into this mess, Andy said to himself with a sense of triumph, and he's going to get me out!

/ Lucas closed his eyes and allowed himself to breathe deeply, even as he pressed his hands together to stop their shaking. When he opened his eyes, nothing had changed. Shelves of neat, dust-free books stood against one wall. The multipaned bay window overlooked a smooth green lawn. The wooden paneling, which covered another wall and bore the antique prints of birds, remained as solid as ever. His stack of mail, opened and unopened, lay before him in neat piles, the daggerlike letter opener near at hand on the desk, the clock radio in the center, the white dial phone on his right. It was the phone that had betrayed him.

"Coincidence," he whispered, berating himself for hanging up so abruptly.

Composing himself, he sat up, adjusted his necktie, picked up his letter opener, shifted his eyeglasses, and selected the next letter. With a deft flick of his wrist he slit the envelope open. It cut across the silence like a muted scream.

/Andy was thinking furiously. Now convinced he would have no problem about getting Lucas to talk to Nina directly, he realized he needed to know how she organized her day, where she went, what she did. Only then could he make sure Lucas met and talked to her at a particular time and place—the best time, the best place.

And perhaps, Andy thought, he could get other people to listen. That would be for later. Nina's schedule was first.

Andy biked to the college.

In the library he quickly checked on the magazine section. An unfamiliar student was behind the desk, sorting volumes. Andy said, "Is Nina Klemmer around?" ready to bolt if she was.

"Not yet."

Andy relaxed. "I need to get her work hours. Got her schedule?"

The student brought out a loose-leaf binder and put it on the counter. "It's in there," she explained.

Since the schedules were listed alphabetically by last names, Nina's was easy to find. "Want to show me how to read this?" Andy asked.

The student was glad to help. "See, she works Mondays through Fridays, four till eight. She'll be here soon."

"What's this on Monday?" Andy said, taking a quick glance at the clock.

The student checked the form. "Oh, right. On Monday she leaves at six. Has a night class in the Old Chapel."

Andy took one of the magazine request forms and wrote down all the information, then left with a quick thanks. It had been so easy. Now, all he needed was the rest of her schedule.

/At dinner that night neither Andy nor his father mentioned Andy's going away. Instead, they talked about sports, the weather, some of Dr. Zadinski's students.

At one point, Andy asked, "How many courses do students have to take?"

"At least four," his father replied. "But most take five. How come you're interested?"

"Just curious."

/ Later that evening Andy heard his father talking to Peggy on the phone. "Andy's much better. It's almost as if he's glad to be leaving, like he wanted me to step in and put a stop to it all. I'm relieved."

Softly, Andy shut the door to his room, sure that his father had no notion of what he was doing.

Around ten Sally called. "Hi, Andy," she said.

"Oh, hi."

"Haven't seen you around much," she said. "Where you been?"

"Just busy."

"Paul said you were going away. That true?"

"Yeah. Well, maybe."

"How come?"

Andy said nothing.

"Andy?"

"What?"

"Do you want to talk about it?"

"No, that's okay."

"Why?"

"It's too complicated to explain. I have to do this alone."

"Do what?"

Again Andy said nothing.

"I just thought I'd call," said Sally.

"Well, thanks."

"When you going?"

"Week or so. Except . . ."

"What?"

"Maybe I won't go."

She waited for him to say more, then gave up. "See you," she said.

"See you."

Andy was tempted to call her back, swear her to secrecy and tell her about his plan. It might be good to test it on someone, to make sure he wasn't overlooking anything. But just as quickly he thought, *This is my show. It has to be mine alone.*

/The next morning Andy got up a half hour before his usual time, dressed quickly, and was just finishing breakfast when his father appeared.

"You're up early," his father said.

"Early Student Council meeting," Andy explained.

"Meetings at eight . . . ," murmured Dr. Zadinski with a shake of his head. He set about making his coffee.

"See you later," Andy called from the door.

"Right . . ." Dr. Zadinski turned to watch him go, pleased with Andy's renewed interest in school.

Instead, Andy went to the college.

/He was not absolutely sure about the daily schedule, but assumed it wasn't that different from high school. Sometimes his father taught an eight o'clock class so he knew when the day began. He was aware that college students didn't go to classes every hour and on some days had no classes at all. He hoped that Fridays weren't such days for Nina.

He reached Whig Hall, where Nina lived, at seven-thirty and easily found a place close to the main door where he would not be noticed, but where he could see anyone who came out.

At ten minutes to eight he noticed a sudden increase in the number of students emerging from the building. They all looked sleepy and several ate as they walked. Nina was not one of them.

Andy took a book from his bag and settled down for a long wait.

Shortly before nine there was another rush of students. And this time Nina appeared, dressed in her usual bright colors, a red dress with high, black boots. She was walking briskly.

As soon as Andy saw her, he dipped his head into his book. But once she passed he rose and followed.

Nina crossed the campus and went into one of the smaller buildings, outside of which was a sign: JOHNSON SCHOOL OF ARTS.

Keeping a safe distance, Andy watched her go into a classroom, then strolled casually by the doorway and took a quick look inside. It was a large room filled with easels, and someone was talking about color. Finding himself a place in the hallway from which he could see the classroom door, Andy waited.

By two-thirty that afternoon he had determined three of Nina's classes. He even knew her lunch hour. She took it in the crowded Student Center and never noticed that Andy was three tables away.

As he sat there he felt almost a delicious sense

of glee. He thought of his father calling him "Sherlock," and rather liked the idea now. Maybe he was more like Spiderman, or rather, Peter Parker watching out for the pretty girl across the way. He was having fun.

Nina strolled across the campus, and Andy kept twelve yards behind, wishing he had a trench coat with a collar to turn up. Then he saw she was heading for Brazell Hall. He stopped, suddenly serious again. The last thing he wanted was a run-in with his father. Just in case, he thought up a story about needing a permission slip, then hurried to catch up.

Nina went directly to the third floor where Dr. Zadinski had his office and where he often taught. Andy kept after her, praying his father wouldn't appear, and when Nina entered a classroom he again took a place that allowed him to see her when she came out.

A few moments before class time Lucas came down the hallway. He passed in front of Andy before entering the same room. Nina was one of his students.

I should have guessed, Andy thought to himself, delighted with his discovery. All the same he felt it was too risky to stay in the building. He got out fast.

Feeling a pang of hunger, he slipped into Minkoff Hall and got a candy bar from a vending machine. Then he positioned himself so he could observe both the entrance to the hall and the library.

A little more than an hour later Andy watched as Nina emerged from the classroom building and went into the library, going, as he knew, to her job.

He had found out her entire schedule.

Given the time left he saw only one choice. Nina had an evening class on Monday night, which went from seven until nine and met in the Old Chapel. It was then and there that Andy had to get Lucas to speak to her.

For a moment, Andy thought of going, too. Just as quickly he realized that would be foolish. It was important for him to keep his distance. Let her hear, on her own, what Lucas had to say.

With a growing sense of excitement and urgency, he decided he'd better start prodding Lucas. He hurried to the Student Center, found a pay phone, and in moments was put through to the Math Department.

"Hello?" came Lucas's voice.

"Zeke?" said Andy. "That you?"

"I think you have the . . ."

"Nina Klemmer," Andy cut in. After a moment of silence he said, "You there, Zeke? This is a message to Zeke from Nina. She wants to meet you."

"Who . . . who is this?"

"Don't you want to meet her?" said Andy, and, worried that he might laugh, hung up. As he left the Student Center he reminded himself that he needed to be free of his father the next day so he could call Lucas again.

/In his office Lucas leaned against the door, preventing anyone from entering. In a sudden rage, he grasped the phone and hurled it against the wall. The phone casing shattered into small, jagged pieces.

/When Andy reached home his father was waiting for him. "How about a movie after dinner," he offered.

"Suits me," said Andy, wondering if his father detected any difference in him. He *felt* different.

Part Four

Dr. Zadinski was done with breakfast, reading the paper, when Andy came into the kitchen. After a while his father said, "Looks like a perfect Saturday. How about doing something together?"

"Can't," said Andy. He set out his own breakfast.

"Why's that?"

"There's a ball game over at Bolton Field. Paul and I want to see it."

"Mind if I tag along?"

"We'd like to go ourselves."

"Andy, you're leaving Tuesday . . ."

"You made those plans. I didn't."

His father studied the paper for a moment, then said, "You are coming to the concert with us tonight, aren't you? I've gotten tickets."

"Got a party," Andy said, though he had no idea what he was going to do other than call Lucas.

"Where?"

"Val Agnew's," said Andy, giving the first name that came to mind.

"Andy . . ."

Andy shook his head.

His father rose from the table and announced he had to go to the supermarket. "Want to come?" he asked.

"Not really," said Andy with a show of indifference. But from the front window he watched his father drive off. As soon as he was out of sight, Andy went to the phone and called Lucas.

"Yes," he heard Lucas say.

"Zeke?"

"This is Dr. Lucas."

"Like I said, Nina Klemmer wants to meet you. How about it?"

Lucas abruptly hung up.

Frustrated, Andy thought: Maybe he doesn't believe me. I could tell him what I know about Nina. . . . The thought made him uneasy. Then he reminded himself it was all for Nina's aid and time was running out.

Next call he'd do better.

/Andy was mopping the bathroom floor when his father returned from the market. "Looks a lot better, doesn't it, Dad?" he said.

Once he was done, he put on his jacket and, for appearances, took along his baseball glove. "Paul says we can grab a sandwich over at his place, then go from there," he told his father.

Dr. Zadinski didn't look happy. "Be back in time for dinner," he said.

"Sure."

"Peggy will be here."

Andy gave a shrug and started to go.

"Hello to Paul," his father called after him.

After watching Andy leave, he turned back into the apartment, unhappy with his own thoughts. All the same, he fetched the town phone book and looked up Paul's number. Rehearsing the excuse he would make—that he

had forgotten to tell Andy he was going out—
he waited fifteen minutes, then called.

/ Andy headed for the phone
booth outside McDonald's. When he reached
it he decided he was hungry and went inside,
working his way through a crowd to get on line.

"Hello, Andrew," he heard.

It was Officer Dorfman. He was out of uni-
form, and a woman and two small kids were
by his side. Andy assumed they were his family.

"Oh, hi," he said, uncomfortable beneath
Dorfman's steady gaze.

"How are things going?" Dorfman asked.

"Fine."

"Sure?"

"Yeah," said Andy, wondering what the man
had in mind.

"Don't forget to let me know when I can be
helpful."

"Thanks," Andy said, wishing he had the nerve
to leave. Instead, he ordered a shake, drank it
quickly, then left. But he was afraid that Dorfman might be watching and rode away without
using the phone.

Andy came upon a number of other phone

booths, but couldn't rid himself of the notion that Dorfman might pass and notice. The thought was so unsettling, he wasn't content until he found a phone in a drugstore.

Lucas answered on the first ring.

Andy said, "I know all about Nina Klemmer, Zeke. She goes to the state college. Lives in Whig Hall. Takes art, English, math, psychology, and a theater class. That math class is yours, Zeke. She's got a red car, an Escort. She's really good-looking and a cool dancer. So are you. I know where you can meet her and she'd like that. Let you know when, okay?"

Lucas said nothing.

"You there, Zeke?"

There was silence.

"That's okay. Long as you keep listening, I'll keep making plans." Andy hung up.

/ It took fifteen minutes before Lucas could ease himself back into his desk chair and attempt to think with any degree of calmness. As it was, his thoughts were a jumble of possibilities—resign from the college, vanish—but the desire to resist, to hold on to the life he had made was strong.

No. Now that he had regained his self-control, he told himself—insisted—that he must not allow this Peter Smith to destroy him. He would fight back as he always had, with cunning as well as strength.

His task was to find him. Lucas cursed himself for tossing out that slip of paper, the one he'd picked up after the departmental meeting. The phone number on it was his only link to Peter Smith.

Quickly, he checked the town phone book. There he discovered a listing for "P. Smith." He called and a woman answered.

"I'm trying to reach P. Smith," Lucas said in his smoothest voice.

"This is Dr. Patricia Smith," came the reply.

"Wrong number," he said. "I am sorry."

Lucas tried to concentrate. Perhaps Peter Smith was a student at the college? He made a mental check of his own students that term. He could recall no one by that name.

He turned to the college phone book. No listing.

The name was probably false.

The voice was that of a male. Not a child—perhaps a male student, a teen-aged male student? Was there anyone Nina Klemmer usually sat with? He could think of no one. Nor had he noticed that she spent time with a particular male about the campus. He would have noticed that.

Idly, he thumbed the corner of the college phone book. A new idea occurred about the number on that dropped slip of paper . . .

When the Math Department meeting had broken up, people had fairly rushed out of the room. Could one of *those* people have dropped it?

If that were the case, it meant he had called someone from his own department!

Lucas flipped open the college phone book and ran down the list of his departmental colleagues and their home numbers. The names ran from Dr. Carlos Boros to Dr. Robert Zadinski. What, Lucas asked himself, did he know about any of them?

For years he had made it his business to gather information about their lives, both public and private. He knew that one of them had a passion for collecting baseball cards. Another prided himself on being an expert on the subject of sea shells. A third suffered serious bouts of depression, another was close to divorce.

It always pleased Lucas to think he knew more

about these people than they ever realized. It gave him power over them, or, at least, the option of power.

Lucas studied their home phone numbers, hoping that one would strike a note in his memory. None did. But who among his colleagues would be calling *him*? Who would ever make the connection?

/ Andy considered going back home but worried that if he did he wouldn't be able to get Lucas again. As he saw it, he had to call Lucas every few hours to keep him on edge, off balance.

In the end he decided he might as well go to Bolton Field in case his father asked questions. But when he reached it, he discovered his father's car in the parking lot.

His first reaction was anger that his father distrusted him, then relief that he'd covered himself by coming.

Hoping not to attract attention, he parked his bike, slipped into the stands, and without looking around leaned back and watched the game as if he had been there all along.

He felt a tap on his shoulder.

"Been looking for you," his father said, climbing onto the bench next to Andy. "Thought I'd like to see the game, too."

Andy kept his eyes on the field.

After a while his father said, "You came alone."

"Paul had something come up."

"That right? When I called him, he didn't know anything about going to a game."

Andy felt his face getting hot.

"And guess what?" his father asked.

"What?"

"He wanted to know if you were feeling any better. Seems you didn't go to school yesterday. That true?"

Andy, not knowing how to answer, said nothing.

"How come?"

"Didn't feel like it."

"Where'd you go? You weren't home."

"Nowhere."

"Andy, from now until Tuesday, all the time you're not in school, we're staying close together. That understood?"

Andy's heart sank.

All he could think about was that he had to get in another call to Lucas. "Let's go home," he said at last.

"Fine with me," his father replied.

"I'll bike."

"I brought the rack," said his father. "Put it on that."

"Just as soon—"

"On the car," his father ordered.

/Andy stared glumly out the side window as they drove home.

After a while his father said, "I'd like to know what you did Friday."

Andy wondered if the question was another test. He decided to take a chance.

"Nothing. Just hung around."

"That's hardly an answer."

Andy kept his mouth shut.

"I picked up your plane tickets earlier," his father said then. "We have to be at the airport about six in the evening."

Andy almost said, "I'll never go," but restrained himself.

"I'm going to miss you," his father said.

"Maybe you won't."

"What's that supposed to mean?"

"Nothing."

"And tonight you'll go to the concert with us. No party."

"What?"

"Call Val Agnew. Say you can't make it."

"No way."

"Andy, the choice is no longer yours."

/ An hour later Andy decided to ask his father if he could go out. Dr. Zadinski was in the kitchen studying a cook book.

"Do you mind if I take a walk?" Andy asked. "I don't feel like staying cooped up like this."

Dr. Zadinski looked at his watch.

"Sure," he said. "We can go. Let me get my jacket."

"Forget it," Andy snapped. He started for his room. "What about calls?" he yelled. "Is that allowed?"

His father didn't even look up from his book. "Call anyone you want," he said.

Andy thought of faking a call to Val Agnew, calling Lucas instead. But he couldn't risk it.

/ Dr. Zadinski cheered up when Peggy arrived. He bustled about the kitchen, full of energy. Andy, with barely a word, flipped on the TV in the living room and tried to concentrate on that. He kept checking his watch, thinking of how little time he had before he'd have to sit down at dinner and listen to their talk. And then the concert after that. . . . He felt like a prisoner.

/ Dinner done, he started on the dishes. "Andy," his father said. "Time to go. You can forget those."

"I'm not going," Andy announced.

"Andy . . ."

"No . . ."

After a moment his father said, "Okay. If you don't want to, that's fine. But then we'll stay home, too."

Andy swung around. "What do you think I intend to do, kill someone?"

"Obviously not. But I don't know what else is on your mind, do I?"

Peggy came into the kitchen. "Andy," she said. "Would it be easier for you all if I weren't around tonight? I can perfectly well leave. I'll understand."

Upset, Andy went to his room without answering and shut himself up.

Within moments his father looked in. "Want to go to a movie?"

"Just leave me alone!" Andy cried.

They did as he asked.

/ Near midnight, his father tapped on Andy's door. "Peggy's leaving," he announced. "You won't see her before you go. She wants to say good-bye."

Hoping his ordeal was over, Andy came out of his room. By the front door Peggy held out a hand. "I hope you have a good time at your aunt's, Andy," she said. "And come back real soon." She stepped forward and gave him a kiss on the cheek. Andy murmured a "thanks," then retreated to his room again.

Once Peggy left, his father looked in. "You weren't very polite."

"She's your friend, not mine."

His father ignored the remark to say, "Got any plans for tomorrow?"

"Am I allowed any?"

"I'm going to bed," his father said.

/ As loudly as possible Andy stepped out of his room, used the bathroom, then went back into his room and turned out the light. But instead of going to bed he re-mained fully dressed and stood by the closed door, listening.

When he thought it was safe he poked his head out of the room, then checked to make sure his father was asleep. Once he was certain, Andy hurried out of the apartment.

/ Lucas answered immediately.

"Zeke?"

Lucas said nothing.

"I'm working out times you can get together with Nina, Zeke. She's right here now. Wants to talk to you. Want to talk to her?"

"I want to talk to you."

"What about?"

"Who are you? Why are you doing this? What do you want?"

The unexpected questions caught Andy off guard.

"Answer me," pressed Lucas. "I need to know."

"Don't worry about it," said Andy, and quickly hung up. For a moment he stood by the phone, puzzled. Why should Lucas question him?

Troubled, he headed home.

/ Lucas bent tiredly over the phone. He had to think.

A meeting seemed to be in the offing. He considered the possibility. What would be its purpose? To attack him? Some kind of blackmail?

The more Lucas considered, the more he realized he would welcome a meeting. The random calls put him at a disadvantage. But with a meeting, he could come prepared to do . . . what?

Teach this Peter Smith a lesson he would never forget. . . .

But that would depend on who was there. . . .

Now that he thought about it, Lucas wondered why Nina Klemmer didn't take the phone when Peter Smith suggested he speak to her. It seemed the reason for the call. Could she *not* have been there? And if she were not there, what did that mean? Would Peter Smith have lied to him?

Lucas decided that if Peter Smith again offered a conversation with Nina, he must take it up. If she *were* part of this, it would mean one thing. If Peter Smith was acting alone, however, it would mean something quite different. It would be so much easier to deal with. . . .

Lucas remained by the telephone, willing Peter Smith to call again, knowing that the more he called, the easier it would be to track him down. Be calm, he told himself, he will call. . . . But it was late, nearly one o'clock. His nervous fingers toyed with the letter opener.

/ Andy rolled over and looked at his clock. He couldn't believe the time: five-thirty in the morning. Despite his tiredness he couldn't get back to sleep.

In less than two days he would be done with it. Nina would be safe. Everyone would know the truth. He couldn't wait.

He tried to find some radio music he liked but nothing was right.

Finally, around seven, Andy got up. His father was still asleep. From the front steps he collected the Sunday paper and read all the comics.

Then he realized he was losing an opportunity to call Lucas. He dressed hurriedly and slipped out.

The day was bright and clear, and promised to be balmy. His father, he knew, would insist they do something together. Andy made up his mind to go along with that.

He went to the nearest phone booth.

Lucas answered on the first ring.

"Hello?"

" 'Morning, Zeke."

"I want you to tell me," said Lucas, "exactly what you want of me. Is it money? Is it something else? I insist you explain yourself."

Andy, taken aback by the force of the questions, was at a loss how to answer.

"I must know what you have in mind," Lucas continued.

"Nina," said Andy.

"What about her?"

"She wants to see you."

"Why?"

"She . . . she likes you."

When Lucas remained still Andy pressed his ear to the phone and heard labored breathing. That time he was certain he had said something right. "Yeah," he went on, "she wants to go dancing with you. Spend time with you. You said you were a great dancer. And, Zeke, Monday you'll be with her at last. Your big chance, right? Tell her exactly what you think of her, okay? I mean, she wants to hear it. How's that grab you? I'll be telling you exactly where and when soon. But don't you doubt it, Zeke, Monday evening. Hey, you there?"

"I wish to speak to Nina."

"Well, she's . . ." Andy didn't know what to say.

"Now," insisted Lucas.

Unnerved by Lucas's insistance, Andy hung up.

What did Lucas want to say to her?

Or was it Zeke who would do the talking?

As he hurried home, Andy wondered what Lucas might actually say to Nina at the Old Chapel on Monday evening. Or—he suddenly stopped—what he might *do*.

He slipped into the apartment to find his father still asleep. Still unsettled, he started making breakfast for them both.

/ "You're in a much better mood," Dr. Zadinski said as Andy put coffee down in front of him.

"It's a nice day."

His father gave him a suspicious look, turned to the newspaper, studied it, then again contemplated his son. "Guess it is," he conceded.

"We should do something," Andy suggested.

"Fine with me. What do you have in mind?"

"Hardy Park. It's open again."

His father set down his cup in surprise. "You kidding? We haven't been there in ages. It used to be your birthday regular, remember? You hated the roller coaster."

"And ask Peggy," said Andy.

"I thought . . . ," his father began, only to stop and look at Andy more closely than before. Andy was aware of the scrutiny. "I did want to be with you," said Dr. Zadinski.

"Go on, ask her," Andy insisted.

"What's all this . . . niceness?"

"I wasn't very polite last night."

"You're right. But you know what?"

"What?"

"When you face up to it, as you're doing, and deal with it straight, hey, we can get past it." He reached out and touched Andy's hand. "I appreciate this," he said.

Andy, knowing he wasn't being completely honest, turned away.

/Lucas had not slept. It was while taking a shower that he thought of something he'd missed: one of his colleagues, Robert Zadinski, recently moved from his house on the outskirts of town into an apartment near the campus. The number in the college phone book was not, therefore, his current number.

As soon as he was dressed Lucas called the old number. After three rings a robot voice came on: "The number you have reached, 771-2441, has been changed. The new number is 771-1416. Repeat: The new number is 771-1416."

Lucas wrote the number down, hung up, and studied what he'd written. The number reminded him of the one he had called, but most of the numbers in Madison were much the same. There were only three phone prefixes. Lucas wasn't sure.

He sat back in his chair. Then it came to him: Zadinski had rushed out of that departmental meeting first. He seemed in a terrible hurry. Could *he* have dropped that slip of paper?

Lucas stared at Zadinski's new number for a long time. To call it, he realized, was enormously risky. If it were the wrong number he could cover himself. But if it were the right one, he couldn't say what might happen. He must not lose control of himself. All the same, he reached for the phone—only to stop in midair.

Bob Zadinski? He couldn't be Peter Smith. . . .

It was incredible even to think it. Besides, Peter Smith's voice was young—and, Lucas realized suddenly, sounded scared.

/The entrance to Hardy Amusement Park was a castle with a drawbridge. Over the gate a grotesque mechanical clown, red-nosed and leering, rocked back and forth, blaring out a hysterical, rolling laugh.

"It hasn't changed in years," said Andy's father, shaking his head.

"Godawful," said Peggy who had not seen it before. She was giggling.

Even Andy felt like laughing.

His father bought strips of tickets good for all rides and handed them out. Then the three of them moved into crowds of parents with young children.

"When was the last time we were here?" Andy's father asked him.

Andy shook his head.

Directly in front of them was the carousel, spinning to the tune of a bouncy waltz. It had all kinds of animals on it, all brightly painted and set in pairs: patient elephants, rearing horses, trotting pigs. Ostriches seemed to race, tigers and wolves to pounce. A pair of lions stalked. Dragons flew and bears pranced.

"You always wanted to ride that first," his father said.

The carousel slowed down and stopped. The man who controlled the ride, high up in a booth, put a microphone to his lips. "Ready to ride, folks! Ready to ride. Pick the animal of your choice for the ride of your life."

It was—Andy remembered—what he had always said.

"There's a flying horse," Peggy cried. "That looks a treat."

"Andy?" his father asked. Unable to make up his mind, Andy studied the animals.

"Take your ride," cried the barker. "Take it now. Into your saddles, please!" He was gathering tickets from those already mounted.

Peggy headed for the winged horse and Dr. Zadinski followed. He attempted to lift her into the saddle, and laughed when he couldn't. She got on herself, sitting sidesaddle, then he took the winged horse next to her.

Andy climbed onto a wolf.

The music began. The carousel swayed, then started to turn. The animals moved up and down.

Andy looked back over his shoulder at his father and Peggy. She was holding out a hand. He took it. Andy turned away, suddenly remembering the last time they'd been there. It was for his twelfth birthday. He had ridden a pig. His father had taken a lion and his mother a blue hippo. He remembered his presents: a new baseball glove from his father and from his mother three cowboy-style flannel shirts, each with white pearl buttons. His grandparents had joined together to give him his first grown-up bike. Aunt Mary had sent books.

Recalling it all with unexpected vividness, Andy felt a deep and sudden grief.

The carousel spun faster. The music bleated. Blinded by tears, dizzy and frightened, Andy wanted to get off but was afraid to show himself weak. Instead he leaned forward, clung to the neck of the wolf, and let himself be carried on.

/ Lucas tried to recall the Zadinski boy. Though his name eluded him, he remembered him from that morning he attended the funeral service for Mrs. Zadinski. It was just about a year ago. And a tragic business.

Once more Lucas saw the stony-faced boy, so unemotional, so cold and unforgiving next to the father so torn with grief.

And now as he thought of it, he was certain he had seen the boy somewhere since. Where? When? he asked himself. He could not place it.

/ "If you want another ride," the barker called, "stay right where you are and have your tickets ready. Have your tickets ready, please!"

Andy quickly got off and composed himself.

"That was *so* much fun," Peggy exclaimed. "Andy, what a fine idea to come. And I do thank you for asking me. Where are we going now?"

A happy Dr. Zadinski turned to Andy and asked him. "Your show, Andy," he said. "Where to next?"

"You go on," Andy replied. "I have to find the men's room."

His father noticed how flushed Andy looked. "You okay?" he asked.

"Fine."

"How about the bumper cars," his father said. "You used to love that. Let's meet there."

Andy agreed and watched them go.

He had dropped one dime into the pay phone when a wave of tiredness passed through him. He considered not calling, letting it all go. Then he thought that if he did stop something would happen to Nina. He would never be able to forgive himself. It was for her, he reasoned, and he dropped in the second dime and dialed.

"Hello?" said Lucas.

"Call you tonight to set the time," Andy said, and hung up quickly, feeling weak, and ashamed of it.

The moment Peter Smith hung up, Lucas was struck by an idea. If he quickly called the new Zadinski number he might catch the boy—assuming he was the one—off guard. He would be right next to the phone and, unthinkingly, he'd pick it up.

Lucas called but no one answered.

Disappointment and relief mingled in Lucas's mind. The truth was, he told himself, the further removed Peter Smith was from the college, the easier, and safer, it would be to deal with him as he deserved.

Andy washed off his face in the men's room and felt calmer for it. Looking into the mirror he scolded himself for his nervousness. To give up would be cowardly. He thought of what Coach Howells had told him: When a ball comes right at you, you don't blink, or duck or retreat. You charge it, catch it cleanly, and whip it across the field for the out.

It's for Nina, Andy told himself. Nina . . .

/ "Great day!" Dr. Zadinski proclaimed as they left the park. At four o'clock they were so tired, not even the mechanical clown, still laughing, made them pause.

Andy's father and Peggy walked hand in hand. Andy followed a step behind.

"I haven't had so much fun in I don't know how long," Peggy said. "Don't you think, Andy?"

"It was fine," he said.

"Let's top it off with a good eat out," said his father.

"Robert," said Peggy, "I'm so sticky and dirty I'm going to have to wash up."

Andy caught the use of the name "Robert." His mother used to call his dad "Rob."

"No problem," said Dr. Zadinski. "We can go

back to the apartment, clean up, and then go. What do you say, Andy? Any place in mind?"

"Wherever."

They drove back to the apartment in silence. Andy sprawled in the rear seat, drifting in and out of a nap. Peggy hummed the whisper of a tune, her voice high-pitched and slow, her arm on the open windowsill, fingers wide to catch the wind. Dr. Zadinski drove with one hand, one arm flung along the seat, fingers drumming to the rhythm of Peggy's tune. His sleeves were rolled up.

From where he lay Andy could see only treetops fly by. He was wondering again what Lucas would say to Nina when they met.

/ Dr. Zadinski opened the door of the apartment, letting Peggy in first. Andy flopped down on the couch.

"I need to wash up something fierce," Peggy announced and headed off.

Andy realized that instead of going to the bathroom she went into his father's bedroom. With hooded eyes he shifted slightly to see what his father would do. Self-consciously, Dr. Zadinski gave a quick look in Andy's direction. Andy shut his eyes and his father followed Peggy.

Andy tried to guess the exact words Lucas would say to Nina. Would he introduce himself as Zeke? No—as Dr. Lucas. How would he dress? Andy wondered. The way he appeared in class, suit, tie, fancy cufflinks? Or would he be different?

And what would he do?

Pulling a pillow over his eyes Andy restated the question. Maybe he *will* be Zeke. Maybe he'll offer to go dancing with her the way he said he wanted to? Maybe he'll play out the whole scene just as he spoke it on the phone?

The memory of the call brought Andy a cold shiver.

What's going to happen? The question really bothered him.

All afternoon Lucas had paced through the rooms of his house, waiting, wanting another call to come. As the hours passed and none did he began to feel like a prisoner. He berated himself that if he gave in to blackmail, this was the way it would always be. Perhaps worse. How could he give in to that? It would leave him no dignity. Lucas grew hot at the thought.

He'd wasted too much time trying to figure out who Peter Smith was. What did it matter? All this talk of a meeting, that was the important thing. Should he go? And if he went, how should he act? He couldn't just go and grovel. And was there even a remote possibility that this Nina Klemmer did want to meet him?

Lucas tried to dismiss that idea as absurd. No, as far as he was concerned the greater likelihood was that this setup was a prelude to blackmail. Money. Or maybe the girl wanted an A for the course. But she was doing fine. Still, he knew of such things. As for money, a teen-ager might not ask for that much. Or too much. No, if some student were behind this, he'd not give in. He had his pride.

It was up to him to show Peter Smith—or whoever—the danger of the game he was playing.

Lucas considered for a moment, then went into the kitchen and pulled open a drawer. Before him lay a row of brilliantly polished, sharp steak knives.

/ There was a hand on Andy's shoulder. He pulled the pillow from his face.

"What?" he said.

His father said, "We're ready."

"Maybe I won't go."

"What do you mean?"

"You two go. I'm not feeling so great."

"What's the matter?"

"Stomach."

"Come on. We'll go to a nice place."

"Dad . . ."

"It's been a great day, Andy. Don't ruin it."

Andy, wishing Peggy wasn't there so he could just talk to his father, said, "Okay. Let me change."

/They got back to the apartment a little after nine. Peggy didn't go in. Instead, she held out her hand to Andy. "Now I really have to say good-bye. It's been a lovely day. Don't worry about things. I'll make sure your father's not too lost." She made a movement to kiss Andy, but prepared this time, he drew back.

"Thanks," he said.

There was a moment of embarrassment, then Andy went in.

Within seconds he heard Peggy's car drive off.

"Really great," his father announced at the doorway. "Now all I have to do is grade papers." He went into the kitchen to make coffee.

Again Andy thought of talking to his father. He decided to clear his head first, think it through. Besides, he was long overdue to call Lucas.

"I need a walk," he said to his father. "You mind?" He realized he wanted his father to tell him he couldn't go.

Dr. Zadinski looked at Andy and smiled. "I think we've both calmed down, haven't we?"

"I suppose . . ."

"Take your walk," his father said. "Just don't wander far. You have school tomorrow."

Andy felt trapped.

"Andy," his father said, sensing Andy's hesitation. "Something up?"

"No, nothing," said Andy, and feeling he had to meet an obligation, he left the apartment.

Lucas answered after two rings. "Zeke?"

"This is Dr. Lucas."

"Tomorrow night," said Andy without enthusiasm. "The Old Chapel on campus. Nine o'clock. Nina will have just finished a class. Get it? Nine at the Old Chapel. Don't disappoint her, Zeke. She really wants to meet you and hear all about you. That clear?"

"Will you be there?"

"What?"

"I want to know if you'll be there."

"I . . . I don't know," Andy stammered, caught off guard. Quickly, he hung up the phone. Why had he said he might be there? He didn't want to be. That wasn't his plan at all. Nina was going to handle it.

But what was Lucas going to do . . . ?

Andy decided he had to speak to his father.

/ Lucas remained at his desk. In front of him were the notes he had taken: the Old Chapel, nine o'clock.

He told himself that it *had* to be someone from the college. Impulsively he dialed Zadinski's new number.

"Hello?"

"Is this Robert?"

"Yes, it is."

"This is Phil Lucas."

"Oh, hello, Phil. How are you?"

"Fine, thank you. Have a moment?"

"Just grading papers."

Lucas sighed. Clearly he was wrong. The boy would not have called with his father right there, would he? Not unless he was calling from elsewhere. . . .

/ Andy returned home ready to talk. But his father was on the phone. When he saw Andy he looked up and waved. Andy, assuming it was Peggy, and certain it would be a long call, as always, felt resentful. He went right to his room and closed the door. No, he would not talk to his father. He would handle it alone as he had planned.

/ "And how are you getting on in your new apartment?" Lucas went on.

"Just fine," said Dr. Zadinski. "Sorry to let the old place go and this is an adjustment. So much smaller. But we're doing well, thanks."

"And your boy . . . ?"

"Andy? Doing fine, too. In fact, we spent the day together at Hardy Amusement Park. Now he's in his room, doing homework. Works hard at school."

"Glad to hear it. Must have been a rough year for him. I'll have you over for dinner some time. Your boy, too."

"We'd like that. . . ."

/ Dr. Zadinski sat back, reflecting about Phil Lucas's call. He was partly amused, partly aware of a tinge of guilt. How could Andy think . . . ? And Phil Lucas didn't invite just anyone to his dinner parties. . . . Dr. Zadinski thought it might be a good idea to tell Andy that Lucas had called, even asked about him. . . .

/ Andy rolled over on his bed and pressed his face into the cool pillow. Lucas is trying to scare me off, he told himself. That's all it is. But maybe if he thinks he's got me scared, he'll think he can hurt Nina—and no one will be the wiser.

As he lay there Andy heard his door open and sensed his father standing over him. Still annoyed with him and no longer wanting to talk, Andy pretended to be asleep.

"Andy?" his father called softly.

Andy made no move.

Retreating, his father shut the door.

/ Lucas stood by the bay window in his study, hands clasped behind his back, staring out into the night. What, he asked himself, had he learned by his call to Bob Zadinski? Zadinski and his boy had spent the day together. He was in his room doing homework. It was proof that Andy Zadinski was not Peter Smith.

The only way he could unmask this caller and protect himself was to show up at the Old Chapel.

What had Peter Smith said? Nina would be taking a class until nine. Yes, Lucas would be there in plenty of time.

He went into the kitchen, retrieved one of the steak knives, and placed it in his briefcase.

/ Andy rolled over. What had Dorfman told him, that it was all talk?

That was the plan. Just talk. As long as Lucas talked to Nina, everything would go fine. Nina would take care of it.

And yet . . .

Andy jumped off his bed and went to search for his father. He had to tell him what was happening. To his surprise he found the apartment dark and his father asleep.

Andy sat on the living room couch, adjusting his eyes to the gloom. The only light came from the outside courtyard lamps and filled the room with odd-shaped shadows.

Now that he thought about it a moment, it was better he hadn't told his father. The result might have been disastrous. His father, in certain rage, would feel he had to do something. Like . . . go to Lucas. And Lucas was an important man. A friend of the college president. Lucas might turn on his father. Make him lose his job. Hadn't his father said Lucas helped him get it? And maybe . . . it would interfere with Peggy.

No. He couldn't tell his father. His father was doing so much better. Andy didn't want to ruin that. Mustn't. He had caused enough problems.

Anyway, he told himself, everything was going to work fine. And . . . if something went wrong, he'd take care of it himself. So, just in case— to protect Nina—he'd better at least think about being there himself.

Andy sat back and closed his eyes. Out of nowhere he heard Mrs. Baskin talking about the boy who cried wolf.

"*Wolf*," Andy whispered to the dark. "*Wolf!*"

Part Five

Andy woke the next morning feeling uneasy. He got up and dressed in five minutes.

He thought once more of talking to his father. But as he put his breakfast together he heard singing from the shower. It was so corny, but Andy hadn't heard that in a year. How could he destroy his father's good spirits? Yes, he had to take care of Nina. But he had to take care of his father, too.

Andy ate quickly, then got ready to leave. "Dad!" he called through the bathroom door. "I'm going!"

"Hold on!" his father called back. "I need to tell you something!"

"Gotta go," said Andy, wanting to avoid him.

"Be out in a second."

Andy left in a rush.

/ He passed a phone booth, then stopped and turned back. It might be a good idea to tell Lucas that he was going to be there just in case he was planning to do anything. . . . As Andy figured it, he could always decide for real later.

When he dropped in his coins and called, Lucas answered instantly.

"Old Chapel at nine, Zeke," Andy said. "Nina is expecting you. So am I."

/ Lucas placed his portable cassette player next to his typewriter, set it to "record," then began to type. Not for long. All he needed was a simple loop of sound.

After carefully taking it apart, splicing the loop, and putting it together again, Lucas dropped the cassette into the machine and turned it on. He was rewarded with the sound

of typing, on, off, the irregular sound of someone hard at work. He shut his eyes and tested
the effect.

He was satisfied.

/ For Andy, the day dragged in-
terminably. He was part of school. He was not
a part.

During eighth period study hall, when he'd
finally begun to concentrate on something other
than the evening, he felt a hand on his shoulder. He jumped. Mrs. Baskin was by his side.

"I think you forgot our appointment," she
said.

Reluctantly, Andy hauled himself up and followed her back to her office.

"I know you're leaving tomorrow," she began
as they faced one another across the desk, "but
I still thought we should talk. Are you looking
forward to going?"

Andy felt like saying, "I'm not going," but
knew he couldn't. "Sure," he said.

Mrs. Baskin held up a large envelope. "I've
collected all your assignments for the next two
weeks. I suggest you check through them tonight and make sure you take the right books."

"Thanks."

Mrs. Baskin studied Andy for some time. "I do think this is a good idea," she said at long last. "We all need vacations. Not everyone is lucky enough to get one when he needs it the most."

"Right," Andy returned, wanting to get up and walk out.

"You know," she continued, "we all care for you around here. When someone we care for is troubled . . . upset . . . we want to help. We don't always know how. The last thing we want is to hurt the people we love."

Andy, increasingly restless, only shrugged.

"You don't think we're doing this because we *don't* love you, do you?"

"Hadn't thought about it."

"Andy, there's an old cliché. You know, that a punishment can hurt the punisher more than the one being punished. Sometimes that's actually true. I think your going away will be very hard on your father."

Andy shut his eyes, wanting not to hear any more. As far as he was concerned they'd had their chance to believe him. Soon they would have no choice.

"Andy?" said Mrs. Baskin. "You're not hearing me. Where are you?"

Andy looked at her glancingly, wondering what she'd say if he told her all that was on his mind. "Nothing," he said.

"Are you sure?"

In the silence that followed Andy admitted to himself that he wanted to talk. But in the same moment he felt it was all too big, too complicated to even begin. How could he start? He had already tried and failed. To talk now would only mess things up when he was on the verge of success. "No," he said to her, "I don't want to talk about it."

"Why?"

Andy closed his eyes. He felt like shouting, "Because no one believes me!"

Mrs. Baskin leaned toward him. "Andy, what is it? Tell me what you're thinking and feeling. It's important. Why are you keeping your eyes closed? What are you seeing?"

Andy stood up. His legs were trembling. "I have to go," he said. "My next class . . ."

Mrs. Baskin sat back with a sigh, then held up the envelope of assignments. "Don't forget this," she said.

At the door Andy paused, wishing she would tell him to sit down. Then he took the envelope. "Thanks," he said.

Andy walked directly out of school, got on

his bike, and went home. He was hoping his father would be there. He thought he'd ask him to go with him to the Old Chapel.

The apartment was empty.

Feeling the need to do something, he fetched his suitcase from the closet and laid it out on his bed. He began to stuff it with clothes, not bothering to fold them.

Why am I packing? he thought to himself. I'm not going anywhere. Everything will be all right. With sudden frustration he took his baseball glove and flung it into his closet.

For a while Andy stood motionless, aware only that he felt cold. He had to talk to someone.

/ Lucas brought his portable cassette player to his college office, plugged it in, and turned it on. Then he stepped outside and closed the door. The sound he heard was not loud, but it was distinct and, as far as he was concerned, perfect.

He turned off the machine and went to teach a class. It was Math 302, the course Nina Klemmer took.

/ "Madison Police. Officer Se-
neto speaking. May I be of some assistance?"

Andy said, "I need to speak to Officer
Dorfman."

"Just a moment, please . . ." The phone
went on hold. Andy was sweating. How to
begin?

"Hello?" said a new voice.

"Is this Officer Dorfman?"

"I'm sorry. He's out of town. Can I help you?"

"Will he be back soon?"

"I really can't say. What was it about?"

"That's okay . . . ," said Andy, and hung up.
He called his school.

"Madison Central High," he heard.

"Mrs. Baskin there?"

"I think she's gone for the day. Let me check."
Andy heard a muffled voice: "Did Ellie just
leave? I thought so. I'm afraid she's gone," the
woman told him. "May I take a message?"

"Can I have her number?"

"It's school policy not to give it out. It's an
unlisted number. I'll be glad to take a message . . ."

Andy hung up and immediately dialed.

"Is Paul there?" he asked.

"Is this Andy? Hi, this is Paul's mother. He's at baseball practice. Paul tells me . . ."

Andy hung up and, feeling almost frantic, called his father.

No one answered.

Andy remained by the phone for five minutes without moving. "I'll tell Lucas it's off," Andy told himself, and called. But after forty rings no one had picked up the phone. He tried Lucas's college number. No one answered there either.

Andy took a deep breath. "I have to go," he whispered, his face in his hands.

/ At last he went to his room and changed into black pants and a deep purple turtleneck. On a piece of paper he wrote a message for his father:

Be back late

and stuck it on the refrigerator door. Then he left.

/ Lucas walked to the front of the classroom. Carefully, he placed his briefcase on the table. Only then did he look up, his eyes darting immediately to the seat where Nina Klemmer usually sat. She was not there. He took it as a bad omen.

With fumbling fingers he unsnapped his briefcase and lifted the lid. The first thing he saw was the knife he had placed there. He snatched out his lecture notes and was bending to latch the case before he realized a student was standing next to him.

"Yes?" Lucas managed to say, wondering if the student had seen the knife.

"Are you going to go over problem twelve?" the young man asked. "I had a lot of trouble with it."

Struggling to regain his composure, Lucas said, "Yes, of course. If you would like."

"Thank you."

As the student turned toward his seat, Nina Klemmer swept into the room. Lucas felt relief. If she were involved it would have been too brazen, too bold, for her to show up that afternoon. Her being there had to mean she had nothing to do with the call.

Something close to joy filled him. He commenced his lecture. . . .

And it was, he thought, a perfect class, complete, lucid, well organized. From his point of view it was a magnificent performance, one that gave him back all his self-confidence.

As he packed up his briefcase he made up his mind: That evening he would proceed as if Peter Smith were acting alone.

/Lucas stepped into the main office of the Mathematics Department and greeted the secretary with a smile. "Would you do me a favor and call the campus security police. Tell them I'll be working in my office late tonight. You know, when the cleaning people come around they might hear me typing. I don't want to be disturbed. It's a big report I have to do. Tell them to ignore me."

/It was almost five when Andy reached the house where he used to live. Straddling his bike, he looked at it from across the street. It was just as it had always been, three stories high, the highest level being the narrow, pitched attic room which had been his. The clapboard exterior of the house was painted light blue, set off by the white of the window sashes, door frames, and front porch. The same curtains hung in the windows.

But the Chevy van in the drive was different. And the lawn—Andy's old job—needed cutting. A turned-over plastic tricycle lay unattended.

As Andy watched, the door of the house opened and two small children came out. They sat down on the top porch steps and began looking through a picture book. To Andy it all seemed wonderfully peaceful, perfect.

/ Lucas took early dinner in the faculty dining room. As he chatted with colleagues he mentioned more than once that he was working late on a report for the President that evening. "No rest for the weary," he said with a smile.

/ Andy checked the time. His father would be home by now. He would have found his note.

He suddenly thought of calling Nina at the library and telling her not to go to that class. Then he realized how stupid that was. That was how it began: Nina would not talk to him. Or listen. No one would.

Across the way the kids got up and went back into the house, slamming the door behind them.

Andy gazed at his old home again, so much the same, so completely different. If you don't keep things from harm, he told himself, they disappear.

It was five-thirty. Andy started off for the college.

/ Lucas set everything up in his office. On a piece of paper he scrawled a note:

Working. Please do not disturb.

Dr. Lucas

He stuck it to his door.

Then he turned on the cassette player. The sound of typing clatter filled the room. That done, he locked the door behind him. For a moment he paused outside and listened, satisfied that it sounded and looked right. Finally, he slipped from the building unnoticed, his briefcase securely under one arm.

/ Andy parked his bike and wandered into the Student Center. It was dinner hour and most students ate in their dorms. Andy, feeling hungry, checked his pockets but found he had brought only seventy-five cents. He got a candy bar.

From one of the couches Andy watched the few students in the atrium, wondering if Lucas was scared. The idea made him feel better—and he thought again that once Nina learned the truth, for herself, she would be safe and the whole business would be over.

His head ached.

/ By six-thirty dusk had come. Andy wanted to wait until six forty-five before moving out, but he found it impossible to sit around anymore.

Forcing himself to go slowly, he left the Student Center. From the main doors he could see the outline of the Old Chapel in its grove of trees. He decided it would be a good idea to check the place out before it became too dark. For all he knew it might have a back entrance. He'd never noticed.

The Old Chapel was triangular in shape, with one tall pointed end like the bow of a ship poking out between the trees. Inside, a light made the old stained-glass windows glow. Once the building had been used for religious purposes. Not anymore. Andy didn't know why.

He studied the bushes on the side facing him, and wondered if he could use them to hide in. Not certain, he made a big circle around to the far side to see if there were others. There were not, but he was glad to find the building had only one door.

Andy studied it carefully. The doorway was partly open. To the left of the door was a bulletin board covered with notices. To the right was a large window through which he was able to see inside.

It was fifteen minutes before seven, time to pick his spot and make sure Nina showed up for class. He decided the best place to watch from was a thicket of trees some forty feet from the entrance. The trees not only provided good cover, they were something to lean against while waiting. He would be able to observe anyone who went in and out, and, for that matter, anyone nearby.

Andy heard footsteps. In the growing darkness he couldn't see clearly who it was, except that it looked like a man.

Andy stood absolutely still.

The man—whoever he was—approached the entry to the Old Chapel and went inside. In moments, more lights went on, including a lamp directly over the door. Inside, the man moved about shifting chairs, then sweeping what looked like a platform.

Andy decided he was the teacher.

Students began to arrive. The first came alone and started a conversation with the man. Then a group of four showed up. Then a couple. Finally, Nina came with another student. She listened intently to what he was saying.

Three more students showed up, the last ones. It was ten minutes past seven by Andy's watch. Inside, the class began.

/ Andy slid to the base of one of the trees, his eyes steadily fixed on the Old Chapel entrance. Except for the light over the doorway, all was dark.

Gradually, Andy realized his tensions had melted away. He understood now it had only been nervousness that things might not work correctly. He smiled to himself. Nina was in class. He was there, waiting. Lucas, he felt certain, would arrive in time. Everything was fine. If anything happened he was there to protect Nina. It would work.

/Waiting proved to be a bore. Andy filled the time by attempting to picture what was going to happen in endless variations. As different as each version was, they all came to the same conclusion: People would admit that he had been right from the start.

It was then he was struck with an odd thought: The only one who believed him was Lucas. And Lucas was the one person he had lied to.

Andy tried to decide how he should react to people when they apologized. Should he tell them "I told you so" or just be modest? He could see himself explaining all the moves, the details. That would be fun.

And at school, how would the story spread? Kids would learn about it. Paul would pass the word. Perhaps there would be a newspaper story about him, his picture on the front page. Well, maybe an inside page. Somewhere. "Madison's own Peter Parker." People would look at him differently. Sally would think more of him, too. The idea made him smile. Oh, he was going to enjoy it all.

/From time to time Andy looked at his watch, holding it up to catch the faint light coming from above the Old Chapel door. Now and again people passed by. When they came, they always seemed to catch Andy by surprise. His first thought was always, Lucas! And he'd jump up in anticipation. But always they walked on by.

He could hear sounds of the class from the Old Chapel. Shouts. Calls. Through the window he saw students moving about. It was an acting class, he decided. He was sure he saw Nina on the stage. He wondered if she ever thought of him.

Andy thought about his father, about how he would explain all that had happened to him. He knew his father would be angry at first, but when the truth came out—the confession from Lucas, the apology from Nina—his father would be proud. So would Peggy, Andy thought. That was good. He sensed she would be around.

It would all work out.

/ At eight-thirty Andy began to consider something new, the direction from which Lucas would arrive. It was very important for him to see Lucas first.

Footsteps.

Andy ducked behind the largest of the trees,

then inched his head around to watch. He was sure it was Lucas and held his breath. But when the newcomer passed by the light, he saw it wasn't. From somewhere behind him, he thought he heard a car. That, too, passed.

Andy stood on his toes and bounced to relieve the tension. It was eight forty-five. He leaned back against the tree and stared into the dark sky. There was almost no moon. He recalled the words of the policeman, "Full moon, Friday night, and welfare checks just out." Andy smiled. Here it was Monday, almost no moon, and all he had was fifteen cents in his pocket.

/ "Do not move. Do not turn around." The voice exploded just behind Andy's ear.

"Nothing!" insisted the voice which Andy recognized as Lucas's. Something sharp prodded his back.

"Take two steps away from the tree," Lucas said. His voice was calm, but hard and low.

Andy did as he was told, trying to twist around to see the face.

"Don't turn," said Lucas, and again Andy felt a sharp prick of pain in his back. He thought his legs would buckle.

"Now," Lucas said, "turn around. I'll be turning, too, behind you. Carefully . . ."

Andy turned, facing away from the Old Chapel, into the dark.

"Now then, Peter Smith . . . lift your hands away from your sides. Good. I want you to walk forward. I will be right behind you." When Andy felt the sharp jab again he realized it must be a knife.

"Go on now," Lucas ordered.

Numb with fear, Andy managed to say, "Where are we going?"

"Not a word," Lucas said curtly. "Walk as I told you!"

Despite his panic, Andy moved forward, occasionally stumbling over uneven ground. "Oh, my God," he heard himself say, "Oh, my God . . ."

"That's it," said Lucas, after they had come some fifty yards through the trees. "Now, move to your right. Stop!"

They had reached the edge of the grove. Andy looked about. A good way off was a dormitory. Equally distant—on the other side— was the library. Before them was a paved service road and a parked car.

"We'll go to the car," Lucas said. "Directly. Do you understand me?"

"I don't want to," Andy pleaded in an almost childlike voice. "I don't."

"Do as you're told," said Lucas. He jabbed Andy again, making him cry out. "Quickly."

Andy, certain he felt blood trickle down his side, did as ordered.

They approached the car. "Lean against it," said Lucas. "Arms over your head. Spread your feet."

Andy was too terrified to argue or resist. Lucas frisked him, then pulled open the front door of the passenger side of the car.

"Get in," he said. "Hurry." He gave Andy a sharp kick to his ankle. Stung, Andy all but fell into the seat.

Lucas pushed the doorlock down, slammed the door, ran around to the other side, and got in. Too late, Andy realized he had lost an opportunity to escape.

"Turn around," said Lucas, pulling Andy's face toward him so he could see it.

Andy could just make out Lucas's expression. He looked as Andy remembered him, composed, trim suit, necktie, hair carefully combed, wearing eyeglasses. Lucas pointed a small flashlight into Andy's face, momentarily blinding him.

"You came to my class, didn't you?" Lucas

said with disgust. He put the flashlight between his teeth, beam aimed at Andy. "Hold your hands in front of you, as if praying."

"Please . . . ," Andy tried.

"Don't talk," snapped Lucas. Andy saw the glint of the knife in Lucas's lap. More frightened than ever, Andy put out his hands. Lucas reached over and twisted a rope he had ready around Andy's hands. Quickly, he tied a knot.

"Now then," Lucas said, "we're ready." He drew a seatbelt around himself and snapped it into the lock.

He started the car, then released the emergency brake between the seats. Lucas turned the car out of the service road and into a parking lot before switching on the headlights. Within moments, they were on the road that circled the campus, then on the main road that led away.

"Where are we going?" asked Andy.

Lucas said nothing.

As they moved out of Madison, Lucas let out a long breath and settled himself into his seat, adjusting the chest restraint slightly. The knife remained in his lap and he gripped the steering wheel with two hands. Passing car lights made his cufflinks flash.

"Now then," Lucas said finally, "tell me about yourself. Peter Smith is not your correct name. What is?"

Andy didn't know what to say.

"Please," said Lucas, speaking calmly. "Do not play games with me. You began this business, but you are in no position to do anything further. I may do as I choose. Is that understood? Now, tell me your real name."

"Andy."

"Last name?"

Andy found it difficult to say.

"Tell me!" barked Lucas.

"Zadinski."

Lucas snapped his head around. "Zadinski?" he said, as if not believing. "Zadinski." Again he looked at Andy, and then the car picked up speed.

Andy stared into the dark. He tried to think of all the things Lucas could do, from turning around and letting him go, to . . . He glanced at the knife, wondering if Lucas meant to kill him. His hands hurt. He had to pee.

At one point, too tired to keep his head up, Andy slumped down. When he did, he realized that the doorlock was close to his mouth. He stole a furtive glance at Lucas. Lucas was staring at the road. With his teeth, Andy pulled the lock up, then stole another look. Lucas hadn't noticed.

It was Andy's first glimmer of hope. But as the car rushed on that glimmer faded.

Andy sensed that the land was no longer as flat as it had been. With increasing regularity hills came. Andy remembered that when Zeke first called, he said he came from where there were mountains.

"Hills here," said Andy. Talking made him feel better. "How far have we come?"

Lucas, as if he'd been in a trance, pulled himself up. "What?" he said.

"Lot of hills," Andy repeated.

"Back there," said Lucas, "at the college, it's all so flat. And even. Nothing changes at all."

Andy turned, wide-eyed, to stare at Lucas. It was not Lucas he was hearing, but Zeke.

"After a while it gets to me," he continued. "I have to get out. Move around. You know, I get restless. Jumpy. If I didn't have the car . . ."

"Did you . . . ," said Andy, almost afraid to ask, "did you really want to kill her?"

"Who?"

"Nina. Nina Klemmer."

"Yeah . . ."

Andy swallowed. "Are . . . are you going to kill me?"

Lucas thought for a long time, never once taking his eyes from the road. "I'm not sure," he finally said.

"My father said . . ."

Lucas turned. "Said what?"

Andy shook his head.

"What?" insisted Lucas.

"If . . . I found you . . . you'd be crazy."

Lucas said nothing.

Andy felt as though his chest was full of stones. "I . . . don't want," Andy stammered, "don't want . . . to be killed. . . . I don't want people to die . . . ever. . . . Just to live." He began to sob uncontrollably.

Lucas turned to look at Andy again but remained silent. They were climbing now and only rarely did a solitary truck pass them by.

/ The car came to a halt. Andy snapped his head out of a doze and looked about. He had no idea how far they had come or where they were.

Lucas pulled up the emergency brake, but kept the car engine running.

Twisting around, Andy could see nothing

but trees on either side of the road. Before them, the headlights poked into nothingness. Andy couldn't, at first, figure that out, then realized they must be on top of a hill, or facing the edge of a cliff. "Where are we?" he asked.

"Gammon State Forest," Lucas answered, setting the gear to neutral even as his hand dropped automatically to touch the emergency brake again.

Andy, very frightened, a pain in his chest, said, "We going to rest here?" He couldn't think what to do.

Lucas didn't answer. He lifted a hand to his forehead and rubbed it lightly. By the dashboard light his cufflinks glinted. "It has taken me years to achieve my life," said Lucas slowly. "Something I made . . . myself. You, with what you have done, would take it all away." He shook his head. "I will not give it up."

Andy couldn't restrain his tears. "It was . . . wrong," he said, "what you were doing . . ."

"I did no harm," said Zeke's voice. "None . . . And you . . ." Lucas's voice, "have done me a . . . great harm." He covered his face with his hands. "A great harm."

But for the softly purring motor, all was still. Lucas breathed heavily, his face hidden.

Without pausing to think, Andy moved fast.

With his bound hands clenched in a fist, he swung about, striking Lucas hard on the forehead. The blow took Lucas by surprise. In the same movement, Andy lunged over, trying to pluck the knife from Lucas's lap.

Momentarily stunned, but trying to hold Andy off, Lucas flung out his arms. But Andy had grasped the knife handle between his fingers and was trying to get a better grip on it. Lucas began beating him, forcing Andy to loosen his hold. The knife slipped to the floor. Lucas reached down and frantically tried to retrieve it. As he did Andy threw himself back against his door, twisting, seeking the door handle. Finding it, he yanked even as Lucas, one hand clutching the knife, tried to hold him back.

Andy threw all his weight against the door. It burst open. Kicking out his legs, Andy began to fall, head first, from the car.

Lucas dropped the knife to the floor and now attempted to grab hold of Andy's thrashing legs. Andy was half in and half out of the car. Lying across the seat, struggling to get a better hold on Andy, Lucas smashed down the emergency brake.

Again and again Andy kicked, trying desperately to squirm away, until one of his kicks struck Lucas in the face and shattered his glasses. Instantly, Lucas pulled back. Blood streamed down his face as Andy flopped out of the car onto his back.

With a violent twist he tried to right himself and gain his feet. As he did, the car began to roll. By the car's interior light Andy saw Lucas pawing at his bloody eyes.

"The car!" screamed Andy. "The car!"

Lucas understood. Though blinded, he sought the door handle, jerked it. The door flew open. Then Lucas tried to get out, but his seatbelt restrained him. Andy watched, horrified, as Lucas frantically fought to find the seatbelt release.

"Get out!" Andy cried. "Get out!"

The car plunged. The twin spears of head-light, pointing down, dropped, then seemed to collapse upon themselves. There was an enor-mous crash. The lights went out and everything became still.

Andy stood listening at the top of the hill. Crickets began to chirp. Lifting his hands to his face, he tried to wipe away his tears. As he did, something fell to the ground.

Andy looked and caught a glitter. When he bent down and picked the object up he discovered it was one of Lucas's cufflinks. In the struggle, he had pulled it off.

Andy clutched the cufflink in his hands and wept. Then, with his teeth he began to tear at the rope. In thirty minutes he had freed himself.

For a while Andy stayed at the top of the hill, looking down to where Lucas and his car had plunged. He was afraid to go close. At last he shoved the cufflink into his pocket and, hoping he remembered the right direction, started to walk.

/ It was almost four in the morning by the time the last of the truck drivers Andy had hitched with dropped him ten blocks from home. As he approached the apartment he saw that the lights were on. He stopped. Once more he went over the story he was going to tell. . . .

His father was sitting on the couch. Peggy was with him. A half-full pot of coffee was on the side table.

Andy's father jumped up. "Where the hell were you?" he cried. "Do you know how worried I've been? My God! The police are out there looking all over creation for you."

"I wasn't anywhere," Andy said. "I was thinking about running away. But I didn't. I was hiding on campus." He hung his head in a show of shame.

Peggy said, "Your dad was awful scared, Andy."

Andy looked up and saw his father's anger fade. Lifting a hand in a gesture of apology, he said, "I mean it. I'm sorry."

For a moment no one said anything.

"Glad you didn't run away," his father said huskily. "Peggy guessed that's what you were thinking about. She also said you'd come back." He approached Andy with open arms and hugged him. "I was scared," he said.

As Andy hugged his father back he felt the desire to tell him what had really happened. But, afraid of the consequences, he resisted it.

"I better tell the police you're here," his father said, rushing to the phone. "How about some ice cream? I've got your favorite kind."

/ Andy spent the day at home sleeping mostly, then packing. Time and again he stopped to think of what had happened, as if he had to live through it repeatedly to be sure it even occurred. Some of it seemed blurry, incomplete, too horrible to be real. He felt numb. Again and again he resisted confessing to his father. And the feeling of victory he thought should be his was not there. What he did feel was loss and terror at the vision of the desperate last moments.

Dr. Zadinski hung about the house, letting Andy sleep. When Andy woke he sat near him and watched the packing.

"Still tired?" he asked Andy.

"A little."

"Don't forget, it should be a little warmer down there."

He asked no question about what Andy had done. Andy was puzzled by this, until—with a shock—he realized that his father was at last believing what he told him.

Early that afternoon Dr. Zadinski went to teach his class at the college. "You going to be all right?" he asked Andy before he left. "I can cancel."

Andy assured him that he would be fine. Without saying so he wanted his father to go to the college and find out what was known about Lucas.

/ When his father came back, about two hours later, Andy woke from a doze.

"Time to get moving," his father said, with a tap on his door.

"I'm up."

Holding himself steady, Andy came out of his room. Dr. Zadinski was in the kitchen drinking coffee.

"You drink too much of that stuff," Andy said.

After a brief hesitation, his father swiveled around and smiled. "Guess so. Get some more sleep?"

"Enough," said Andy, searching his father's face for some clue to his thoughts. He saw nothing. "What time do we have to leave?" he asked.

"Four-thirty. We'll eat at the airport."

Andy sensed his father was hiding something and turned away. "Do I have time to take a shower?"

"Better make it quick."

／At four-thirty he stood by the front door, his packed suitcase and book bag at his feet.

"Got everything?" his father asked.

"Think so."

"All your schoolbooks?"

"Sure."

"Baseball glove?"

"I'm not going to play . . ."

"Maybe you will. Keep in shape for when you get back. I'll get it," he said, starting to go.

"Suit yourself," Andy said. As his father left the room Andy was more certain than ever that he'd heard something about Lucas at the college. He wondered if his father would tell him, and if he could keep from giving away the truth. More than anything Andy wanted not to hurt his father now.

／Dr. Zadinski walked into Andy's room and smiled at the familiar mess. It seemed an indication of normality. He looked about for the baseball glove, but when he didn't see it, he opened Andy's closet. The glove was lying on the floor next to the heap of clothes from the night before.

Dr. Zadinski bent down to pick up the glove. As he did he caught sight of something metallic. He picked up the glove, transferred it to his left hand, then reached for the object that had caught his eye.

It was a cufflink.

Puzzled, Dr. Zadinski examined it. He saw that the ornate gold design on the top of the cufflink was made of the letters "P.L."

It took a moment for him to realize what that meant, but once he did, a look of horror overcame his face. Quickly, he shoved the cufflink into his pocket—only to take it out again, as if doubting his senses.

"Better go!" Andy called from the front room.

Again Dr. Zadinski pocketed the cufflink, then emerged from Andy's room, baseball glove in hand.

"Here it is," he said. He bent down so he could avoid looking at Andy and poked the glove into the book bag. His face composed, he stood up. "We better go," he said.

The ride to the airport passed in silence. Andy gazed at the scenery, feeling once more the desire to tell his father everything that had happened. But again he suppressed it, thinking of all that *might* happen. His father would be devastated.

From time to time Dr. Zadinski took his eyes from the road to steal a glance at Andy, looking at him as if he were an entirely new person, a stranger.

He said nothing. He was afraid to.

/ At the airport, they checked Andy in at the ticket counter, received his seat assignment, and went to eat.

During dinner they talked about nothing in particular, the weather, sports, trips Dr. Zadinski had made, stories about Aunt Mary. Andy kept wishing he could find some way of pleasing his father. Finally he said, "You really like Peggy, don't you?"

"Yes, she's a good person."

"She makes you feel good," said Andy. "I like her."

Taken by surprise, Dr. Zadinski gave Andy a grateful look. "You do?" he said.

"Really. You make a nice pair."

"I'm glad you feel that way."

Andy checked the time. "It's getting late."

Dr. Zadinski studied his plate. "Andy . . . ," he began.

"What?"

"Nothing. Let's go."

*They found seats in the waiting lounge. Andy could tell his father wanted to say something. He wanted to hear, but was afraid of it. He pulled a book from his bag.

His father heaved himself up into a straight position. "Andy . . . ," he said. "I suppose I should tell you."

Andy braced himself. "What's that?" he said, trying to sound nonchalant.

"Dr. Lucas . . . Phil Lucas . . . you know. The one you thought . . . you said he made that call."

Andy had been staring at the rug. Now he forced himself to face his father. It was Dr. Zadinski who looked away.

"Last night," his father continued, his voice low, "Dr. Lucas was killed in a car accident."

"That so?"

"Miles from Madison, way up north. In the hill country. I think that's where he originally came from. No one knows what he was doing up there. He has no family left. Awful poverty up there. Always been that way. No one knew he had gone. In fact, he told people he was going to work late in his office. But, in his office—this is what I was told—he had set up a cassette player, sort of a loop thing which made it sound like he was typing in there.

Seems . . . at least people are speculating . . . that it was suicide." Dr. Zadinski put his hand in his pocket. "No witnesses of course. But there was a note on his door saying he was working late. That's all. Nothing to explain . . . anything."

Andy, chilled by his father's words, realized that Lucas must have meant to set up an alibi so he could kill him. "Too bad," he managed to say.

Dr. Zadinski kept his face averted. But when he'd finished he took his hand out of his pocket and shifted about so the two of them finally looked into one another's eyes.

Andy, sensing only unasked questions, unstated pain, remained steady.

"Yeah." Dr. Zadinski, to Andy's relief, turned away. "Nice guy. You know, he called me Sunday night."

"He did?" said Andy, tightly squeezing the book he pretended to be interested in.

"Yes, something about new courses. I meant to tell you. But you were already asleep. In fact, he asked about you. Wanted us to come for dinner. . . . He'll be missed. There'll be a memorial service, I guess." Dr. Zadinski took a deep breath and again put his hand into his pocket. "I guess . . . it's not nice to say . . . but, maybe, it'll make you . . . I don't know . . . rest easier."

"Really," said Andy.

/The final boarding call was made. Andy and his father stood up.

"Hey," his father said, "I'm going to miss you. And you know what . . . ?"

"What?"

"It's been one rough year. The whole thing. But Andy . . . I think we've grown . . . well, stronger . . . closer . . . more caring for each other. Right? Maybe that's what it's all about."

It took more and more effort for Andy to hold himself together. "Right," he whispered back.

"How about a hug?" his father said, taking an empty hand from his pocket as he reached for Andy.

They hugged.

"Love you," said Dr. Zadinski into Andy's ear.

Andy couldn't speak.

/From one of the large airport windows, Andy's father watched the plane as it waited at the head of the runway, heavy and still. Lights flashed at its wingtips. Slowly, the plane began to move, then faster and faster until its nose lifted. Graceful, beyond weight, it seemed to leap into the air.

/ Andy looked out the plane window. The ground was rapidly dropping away. As they climbed higher, the sky ran with the endless red lines of sunset.

Andy wondered if his father would ever guess what had happened. No, he could not. And to himself, he swore that he would never tell because it would kill his father and Andy knew how much he needed him and loved him. No, he would never tell.

/ As Dr. Zadinski left the airport terminal, he dropped the cufflink into a trash barrel. It was wet with tears.